1981

EXTERMINATO

University of St. Francis
GEN 813 B973e
Burroughs
Exterminator

3 0301 00028297 6

S0-BRH-921

Also by William S. Burroughs

Junkie

Naked Lunch

Nova Express

The Soft Machine

The Ticket That Exploded

The Wild Boys

Yage Letters (with Allen Ginsberg)

The Last Words of Dutch Schultz

EXTERMINATOR!

A NOVEL BY

WILLIAM S. BURROUGHS

A Richard Seaver Book

The Viking Press   New York

LIBRARY
College of St. Francis
JOLIET, ILL.

LIBRARY
College of St. Francis
JOLIET, ILL.

Copyright © 1966, 1967, 1969, 1973 by William Burroughs
All rights reserved
A Richard Seaver Book/The Viking Press
Viking Compass Edition
Issued in 1974 by The Viking Press, Inc.
625 Madison Avenue, New York, N.Y. 10022
Distributed in Canada by
The Macmillan Company of Canada Limited
SBN 670-30281-3 (hardbound)
    670-00575-4 (paperbound)
Library of Congress catalog card number: 72-9736
Printed in U.S.A.

Second printing November 1974

Portions of this volume have been previously published,
in somewhat different form, in the following places:
Antaeus, Atlantic Monthly, Cavalier, Daily Telegraph (London),
Esquire, Evergreen Review, Mayfair, Rolling Stone, The Village Voice.

Acknowledgment is made to Warner Bros. Music for lyrics from
"Ain't She Sweet." © 1927 Advanced Music Corporation.
Copyright renewed. All rights reserved. Used by permission
of Warner Bros. Music.

LIBRARY

LIBRARY

CONTENTS

813
B973e

EXTERMINATOR!

95556

"EXTERMINATOR!"

"You need the service?"

During the war I worked for A. J. Cohen Exterminators ground floor office dead-end street by the river. An old Jew with cold grey fish eyes and a cigar was the oldest of four brothers. Marv was the youngest wore windbreakers had three kids. There was a smooth well-dressed college trained brother. The fourth brother burly and muscular looked like an old time hoofer could bellow a leather lunged "Mammy" and you hope he won't do it. Every night at closing time these two brothers would get in a heated argument from nowhere I could see the older brother would take the cigar out of his mouth and move across the floor with short sliding steps advancing on the vaudeville brother.

"You vant I should spit right in your face!? You vant!? You vant? You vant!?"

The vaudeville brother would retreat shadowboxing presences invisible to my goyish eyes which I took to be potent Jewish Mammas conjured up by the elder brother. On many occasions I witnessed this ritual open mouthed hoping the old cigar would let fly one day but he never did. A few minutes later they would be talking quietly and checking the work slips as the exterminators fell in.

On the other hand the old brother never argued with his exterminators. "That's why I have a cigar" he said the cigar being for him a source of magical calm.

I used my own car a black Ford V8 and worked alone carrying my bedbug spray, pyrethrum powder, bellows and bulbs of fluoride up and down stairs.

"Exterminator! You need the service?"

A fat smiling Chinese rationed out the pyrethrum powder—it was hard to get during the war—and cautioned us to use fluoride whenever possible. Personally I prefer a pyrethrum job to a fluoride. With the pyrethrum you kill the roaches right there in front of God and the client whereas this starch and fluoride you leave it around and back a few days later a southern defense worker told me "They eat it and run around here fat as hawgs."

From a great distance I see a cool remote naborhood blue windy day in April sun cold on your exterminator there climbing the grey wooden outside stairs.

"Exterminator lady. You need the service?"

"Well come in young man and have a cup of tea. That wind has a bite to it."

"It does that, mam, cuts me like a knife and I'm not well you know/cough/."

"You put me in mind of my brother Michael Fenny."

"He passed away?"

"It was a long time ago April day like this sun cold on a thin boy with freckles through that door like yourself. I made him a cup of hot tea. When I brought it to him he was gone." She gestured to the empty blue sky "Cold tea sitting right where you are sitting now." I decide this old witch deserves a pyrethrum job no matter what the fat Chinese allows. I lean forward discreetly.

"Is it roaches Mrs Murphy?"

"It is that from those Jews downstairs."

"Or is it the hunkys next door Mrs Murphy?"

She shrugs "Sure and an Irish cockroach is as bad as another."

"You make a nice cup of tea Mrs Murphy . . . Sure I'll be taking care of your roaches . . . Oh don't be telling me where they are . . . You see I *know* Mrs Murphy . . . experienced along these lines . . . And I don't mind telling you Mrs Murphy I *like* my work and take pride in it."

"Well the city exterminating people were around and left some white powder draws roaches the way whiskey will draw a priest."

"They are a cheap outfit Mrs Murphy. What they left was fluoride. The roaches build up a tolerance and become addicted. They can be dangerous if the fluoride is suddenly withdrawn . . . Ah just here it is . . ."

I have spotted a brown crack by the kitchen sink put my bellows in and blow a load of the precious yellow powder. As if they had heard the last trumpet the roaches stream out and flop in convulsions on the floor.

"Well I never!" says Mrs Murphy and turns me back as I advance for the *coup de grâce* . . . "Don't shoot them again. Just let them die."

When it is all over she sweeps up a dustpan full of roaches into the wood stove and makes me another cup of tea.

When it comes to bedbugs there is a board of health regulation against spraying beds and that of course is just where the bugs are in most cases now an old wood house with bedbugs back in the wood for generations only thing is to fumigate . . . So here is Mamma with a glass of sweet wine her beds back and ready . . .

I look at her over the syrupy red wine . . . "Lady we don't spray no beds. Board of health regulations you know."

"Ach so the wine is not enough?"

She comes back with a crumpled dollar. So I go to work . . . bedbugs great red clusters of them in the ticking of the mattresses. I mix a little formaldehyde with my kerosene in the spray it's more sanitary that way and if you tangle with some pimp in one of the Negro whorehouses we service a face full of formaldehyde keeps the boy in line. Now you'll often find these old Jewish grandmas in a back room like their bugs and we have to force the door with the younger generation smooth college trained Jew there could turn into a narcotics agent while you wait.

"All right grandma, open up! The exterminator is here."

She is screaming in Yiddish no bugs are there we force our way in I turn the bed back . . . my God thousands of them fat and red with grandma and when I put the spray to them she moans like the Gestapo is murdering her nubile daughter engaged to a dentist.

And there are whole backward families with bed-bugs don't want to let the exterminator in.

"We'll slap a board of health summons on them if we have to" said the college trained brother . . . "I'll go along with you on this one. Get in the car."

They didn't want to let us in but he was smooth and firm. They gave way muttering like sullen troops cowed by the brass. Well he told me what to do and I did it. When he was settled at the wheel of his car cool grey and removed he said "Just plain ordinary sons of bitches. That's all they are."

T.B. sanitarium on the outskirts of town . . . cool blue basements fluoride dust drifting streaks of phos-phorous paste on the walls . . . grey smell of institu-tion cooking . . . heavy dark glass front door . . . Funny thing I never saw any patients there but I don't ask questions. Do my job and go a man who works for his living . . . Remember this janitor who broke into tears because I said shit in front of his wife it wasn't me actually said it was Wagner who was dyspeptic and thin with knobby wrists and stringy yellow hair . . . and the fumigation jobs under the table I did on my day off . . .

Young Jewish matron there "Let's not talk about the company. The company makes too much money anyway. I'll get you a drink of whiskey." Well I have come up from the sweet wine circuit. So I arrange a sulphur job with her five Abes and it takes me about two hours you have to tape up all the windows and the door and leave the fumes in there 24 hours studying the good work.

One time me and the smooth brother went out on a special fumigation job . . . "This man is sort of a crank . . . been out here a number of times . . . claims he has rats under the house . . . We'll have to put on a show for him."

Well he hauls out one of those tin pump guns loaded with cyanide dust and I am subject to crawl under the house through spider webs and broken glass to find the rat holes and squirt the cyanide to them.

"Watch yourself under there" said the cool brother. "If you don't come out in ten minutes I'm coming in after you."

I liked the cafeteria basement jobs long grey basement you can't see the end of it white dust drifting as I trace arabesques of fluoride on the wall.

We serviced an old theatrical hotel rooms with rose wallpaper photograph albums . . . "Yes that's me there on the left."

The boss has a trick he does every now and again assembles his staff and eats arsenic been in that office breathing the powder in so long the arsenic just brings an embalmer's flush to his smooth grey cheek. And he has a pet rat he knocked all its teeth out feeds it on milk the rat is now very tame and affectionate. I stuck the job nine months. It was my record on any job. Left the old grey Jew there with his cigar the fat Chinese pouring my pyrethrum powder back into the barrel. All the brothers shook hands. A distant cry echoes down cobblestone streets through all the grey basements up the outside stairs to a windy blue sky.

"Exterminator!"

THE LEMON KID

As a young child Audrey Carsons wanted to be writers because writers were rich and famous. They lounged around Singapore and Rangoon smoking opium in a yellow pongee silk suit. They sniffed cocaine in Mayfair and they penetrated forbidden swamps with a faithful native boy and lived in the native quarter of Tangier smoking hashish and languidly caressing a pet gazelle.

His first literary exercise was called *The Autobiography of a Wolf*. People laughed and said: "You mean the biography of a wolf." No he meant the *auto* biography of a wolf and here is the autobiographical wolf and his wolf mate Jerry the red-haired wolf in a cool limestone cave licking the sheep blood off each other they are covered with it from head to foot it's been a great night with the sheep and they laugh at those stupid ranchers and often carried poisoned meat for miles in their jaws and flip it into ranch yards to kill the yapping yellow-toothed wolfhounds. As the sun rises they huddle against each other and fall asleep with contented belches.

The idyl ends. Jerry falls to a bounty hunter's bullet. Saddened by the loss of his wolf mate and weakened by distemper Audrey is run down and eaten by a grizzly bear. Now Audrey knew that bears are largely vegetarian and certainly would not eat such a sick skinny grey wolf as Audrey autobiographically was but would simply fold him in warm paws and promise him suitable wolf mates in Moscow so the end rang as false as a Communist mural. Audrey takes off his wolf suit and works on a collective farm. There he is sloshed on a tractor singing "Ochi Chorniya." Better he should have died with his wolf mate from a bounty hunter's bullet.

Jerry the red-haired wolf reappeared years later as the Lemon Kid. He arose from a conversation in which Audrey was not quite included as he usually wasn't he was known simply as "the sheep-killing dog" at Los Alamos where they later made the atom bomb it seemed so right somehow.

"So the sax player sees this guy in the front row sucking a lemon and . . . ARGURGLUUBURK . . ." (imitation of sour note on the sax).

"You mean?" Audrey inserted.

"Sure. Just the sight of someone sucking a lemon will do it."

Audrey sidled away having heard what he was there to hear. That night in bed with his eyes closed the pictures came and Audrey knew he was going to have a character.

He is in an East St Louis night club. The band is playing "Ain't She Sweet" with a female vocalist and it's terrible. Audrey covers his ears. Suddenly the Lemon Kid stands in front of the orchestra. He has a straw-colored face dusted with orange freckles and bright red hair.

"Ain't she sweet
See her coming down the street . . ."

He listens and his lips draw back from his teeth.

"Now I ask you very confidentially . . ."

He slips half a lemon into his mouth and sucks it around in circles gurgling through the lemon from deep in his throat.

"AIN'T SHE SWEET . . ."

A crescendo of sour notes from sax and horns. The vocalist stands there with spit hanging off her chin like a cow with the aftosa. Waiters and bouncers converge. The Lemon Kid spits out his lemon, drops on all fours and turns into a skinny red-haired wolf smiling his back teeth bare as he leaps through a window into the summer night. The Lemon Kid went on to demolish hymns, national anthems, Irish tenors, yodeling cowboys and individual atrocities like "Trees" and "Danny Deaver." At a Wallace Rally he put the lemon on Old Glory. There he is right in front of the orchestra a raccoon skin coat down to his ankles carrying a YOUTH FOR WALLACE banner.

"OH SAY CAN YOU . . ."

He pops the deadly lemon into his mouth and lisps through it . . .

"THEEEEEEEEEEEE"

The orchestra disintegrates in sour notes and pathic screeches from the horns. Now he turns to the singing audience and shoves his lemon in every bellowing mouth. He spits out the lemon strips off his raccoon coat and stands naked with a hard-on. A cry of strangled rage bursts from the crowd screaming clawing slipping on their spit to get at him as he drops on all fours smiling his back teeth bare and ejaculates canines tear through his bleeding gums stretching his face to a snout red hair ripples down his back into a bushy red tail laps his lean flanks leaner crinkles and shrinks his balls squeezing jets of sperm from his red pointed wolf phallus quivering teeth bare his eyes light up bright lemon yellow and nitrous fumes steam off his body a reek of burning film and animal musk. He leaps through an invisible window and disappears in the 1920 night with a distant sour train whistle.

When the Kid puts the lemon on you you are through in show biz. Time to retire. Get half a sucked lemon spit out on the ground as he smiles all his teeth at you and skitters away across a distant sky.

Packing quickly. Must leave for water. Whistled in the shadow. Wait for Monday sadness. I was talking to someone vague. My suitcase. Farja waits. Hadn't any more. Long overdue. I tell him I have no time. Points after his master there. Breaks into tears. Now from the doorway it is grey in the snow. Dumbbell the pointer. Teeth. He is trying to smile. I hadn't thought of dumb half-healed scar on the right a wall. Luster of stumps washes his way. Cold lost marbles in the night. Little blue-eyed twilight flicker of weeds from vacant lots. Blue stars alleys in the sky. Withered brown plants in pots. In ten minutes June 15 me at the detour. Crumpled stars. CIA agents faded in a mirror.

Has gone. Alie arrives on the blue boat. Pale smoke boy. Is nothing there. I can see a dog pointing with fur like a wolf. It shows gold. He is sick and injured. Ice skates on side of his head. Grins between his legs. Blue stars in the sky. Go there soon?

Come and jack off . . . 1929
little boy did.
smell of attic room musty darkness
a black dog comes down the stairs
caught a glimpse of the Canadian army
blizzard blowing rainbow death mask
ass . . . showers . . . the bunks were empty
birch lots . . . cool evening sky
in the plane I realized what had happened
a skull his name.
saying something lips chapped
standing at the window . . . forget-me-nots
a room haunted by cold coffee . . . summer people
little post card town ghostly young face
yellow perch flapping on the pier
smell of urine on moss
and here is Snowy Joe his face twitching
he needs the Snow
silent snow secret snow on grimy back stairs
blowing under rooming house doors
blanketing back yards and ash pits
Come and jack off . . . 1929
smell of musty summer in the distance
little boy did very little
chapped lips yellow urine on moss
smell of caramel cake on his breath

room with ship scenes on the wall
a dusty sea shell in the empty room
a side porch in Cambridge
Doctor Benway drunkenly
added two inches to a four-inch incision
with one stroke of his scalpel
and he was there like the Lemon Kid.

SHORT TRIP HOME

The face of the pitchman is "helpless yet brutal, unhopeful yet confident . . . powerless to originate activity, but infinitely capable of profiting by a single gesture of weakness in another . . . eyes of an animal sleepy and quiescent in the presence of another species . . ." From *A Short Trip Home* by F. Scott Fitzgerald.

"Step right up for the greatest show on earth. The biologic show. Any being you ever imagined in your wildest and dirtiest dreams is here and yours for a price. The biologic price you understand money has no value here . . ."

"We paid to get in didn't we?"

"Well it's usual to pay isn't it?"

A room with rose wallpaper smoky red sunset two red-haired boys looking at each other turn redder cocks sway and stiffen a musky odor fills the room and drifts out on the still hot air . . . (Scattered coughs from the audience) . . . The nipples of one boy disappear in swirls of nitrous vapor leaving two pearly vibrating disks . . . (The audience stirs buttoning jackets shoving hands in pockets) . . . The boy's face gathers a reptilian concentration . . . a loud snap crackling sounds and broken bottles set in the wall. Glad tidings in my ear spoke of his silent dogs stained with blood and wind of this lonely city a schoolboy screaming for asylum. Are you willing and able to pay the price? Not that way. Transistor radio giving that pass. Shine Boy telling you go back to the big market . . .

"Now some of you may have noticed a strange smell emanating from these characters . . . a sweet rotten musky nitrous ozone smell like a fox den in a photographic dark room . . ."

The other boy sways dizzily his face torn by naked lust and pain red orange yellow vapors steam off him his nipples swell erect quivering burning he falls on the bed and with a quick inhuman leap the other lands on the bed and shoves his legs apart the rectum quivering lined with red frog eggs and the smell reeks out of them as they fuck . . .

"Yes it acts like cyanide on a tight white Rightie . . ."

The sheriff and his pig-faced deputy and the Anti Obscenity League turn blue and flopping around shitting and pissing on the ground . . .

"Now children generally like this smell and come out in red blotches and say 'Gee you can keep me here as long as you like as long as you give me these . . .' "

The boys are coming now teeth bare eyes burning hair bristling . . . red animal hair sprouts all over their bodies canines tear through bleeding gums a boy shivers and kicks asshole vibrating as a tail sprouts out his spine . . .

DAVY JONES

"Young boys need it special."

An adolescent stands with his fly sticking out and pimples explode all over his face.

Here is Audrey at 14 fear and uncertainty written across his face that most people instinctively dislike and distrust. He looks like a sheep-killing dog with sheep blood all over his face wagging his tail at the same time ready to snap or take to his heels. On Saturdays he would go down to the courthouse and sit in on trials the smell of stale sweat and cigar smoke brings it all back how Audrey quailed under the cold eyes of cigar-smoking detectives.

Audrey has slunk into the courtroom and forgot to take off his hat.

"TAKE OFF YOUR HAT."

He sits down shattered as was his usual condition. He turned and looked to his right. Sitting on the second bench ahead of him was a black man one elbow over the back of the bench. Audrey stared at the man who could easily have seen him out of the corner of his eye. If he was aware of Audrey's scrutiny he gave no sign. What held Audrey open mouthed was the immediate knowledge that this man was not moving *inside* not moving one fraction of an inch for anybody and his physical immobility accumulated a power that Audrey could feel like an electrical force field. And now a case was called.

"DAVY JONES."

A boy of about 15 escorted by a bored cop stood in front of the judge. Looking back I see something like a stage with a suggestion of curtains. As his name is called Davy Jones walks in from the left. He is 15 powerfully built and tall completely relaxed and sure of himself he stands in front of the judge with an insolent smile. Audrey realized that the *boy was fearless.* He licked his lips and started to get a hard-on.

"I'm not guilty" said the boy saucily.

The judge moved back. He shied back his fat flesh retreating. "You *are* guilty. You've been *found* guilty and I'm sentencing you to 5 years in Boonville."

BOONVILLE . . . Audrey buttoned his coat to cover his crotch. He remembered a newspaper story about boys held in the city prison awaiting transfer to the reformatory at Boonville, Missouri . . . complaints of "loathsome actions of the boys performed at the dormitory windows in plain sight of passers-by." . . . He saw himself in a cell with Davy Jones . . .

"I'm not guilty" the boy said again smiling openly contemptuous.

"Any relatives in the courtroom?" the judge asked.

The black man spoke from the bench . . . "I'm the boy's father. He's not the type to do that." He did not move or change his position. His voice fell in the courtroom as flatly insulting as hard black knuckles across the judge's face.

The judge blinked and moved back . . . "He *is* the type . . . He's been found guilty of armed robbery . . ."

"He's not the type."

Audrey realized that the judge was afraid of this man. The judge and the bailiffs as well. Nobody told him to stand up or address the court as your honor.

Years later in New Orleans while in jail on narcotics charges he met another black of the same quality. He was known as Clutch because of a deformed hand. He was skeleton thin composed cool and aloof with the other prisoners. And insolent to the narcs.

"Old monkey climbing up on your back boy?" said a narc clapping him jovially on the back.

"I don't know what you're talking about now" said Clutch coldly.

The narc dropped his hand and turned away coughing. Why did they take it from him? Because they were afraid of him. Davy Jones father and son and Clutch destroy the whole white world.

THE EVENING NEWS

The old desk sergeant looked grimly at the wanted
pictures yellow pealing
30th day without an arrest in New York area
they risk 15 light-years, entire future,
certain discussions, cool gardens and
pools of the evening.
The old turnkey makes the round of empty cells.
"Sleep tight boys."
No one there
muttering phantom voices
peet men junkies con men
the old hop smoking worlds
mutter between years.
The Sailor hanging by his belt
A drunk banging on the door of his cell
thin grey pickpocket stops him.
"Get me this letter out, Screw.
It's worth an Abe to you."
pulls the Abe out of his fibrous junkie shoe.
"I need an arrest, Mike. I'm thin."
"Fuck off punk
I can't find an old drunk."

No arrest. She reads it in his dull eyes.
"Conservez toujours une bonne morale."
a sharp cold bray of laughter
sliding away into the sky
"Cher ami, voici mon dernier livre."
Couldn't reach from the old cop film.
Twirling his club down cobblestone streets
the sky goes out against his back
in a darkening park
couldn't reach with the sap
"et personne n'a ri"
I do not need to remind you
laws as strict as the United States . . .
urine in straw a yellow sky
his bicycle of light
"poumons sensibles."
a blue smell of hope as he rounded the corner
and the sea air hit his face
"Leaving the fading film please."
Got up. Remembered "Thank you."
The Old Courthouse empty cells and precincts
bondsmen judges lawyers probation officers
paper cups of coffee on the desk
NARCOTICS DEPARTMENT . . . the door is open
files and pictures scattered on the floor
stained with urine and excrement.
On the wall in phosphorous roach paste
AH PUCH JACKED OFF HERE.
Laws as severe as the United States,
"L'indécision ne servirait pas votre cause ce soir."

ASTRONAUT'S RETURN

Walking along Ladue Road with his father white
frame buildings yards overgrown with weeds and
vines Peter rose thirty feet in the air he had hoped
to surprise his family showing them how he could fly
but his father only looked sad knowing that Peter
would not stay now the scene shifted ground and as-
phalt turning soundlessly Peter was in front of the
J.B. school much smaller than he remembered it con-
struction work on the building abandoned smell of
empty summer classrooms phantom voices walking up
the hill to the house on Price Road which was also different than he remembered it up the back stairs to his
room an open window on the top landing he could see
moss and grass growing through broken stone of the
window ledge his room had been partitioned across
the lights would not turn on from the wall switch there
was a round panel on the table with a switch that
turned on small lights strung about the room the fes-
tive lights for his return dim and dreary in the dark
room a musty smell of disuse the partition formed a
separate room a window opening on the wooded valley
he remembered was clouded over as if seen through

tears he noticed that his hands were torn and lacerated turning back through the games and falls brambles and cuts of his childhood his father there with the iodine he was indifferent to the stings and he could tell by his father's face that this indifference this refusal to play the old game of "ouch" was a final sentence of separation. Peter was thinking that he would have to shave putting it off remembering the parties and the people he used to know thinking how little point there was in seeing any of them now frayed distant voices he walked to the window and looked out feeling his father's sadness behind him the cold emptiness of space between them exploded star between them. What had happened to the glass? It appeared to have been partially melted. He would have to shave stubble of beard on his face he had come a long way to this house sad dead empty he spit out some chewing gum into a toilet bowl and looked around listlessly for a razor and shaving soap.

According to ancient legend the white race results from a nuclear explosion in what is now the Gobi desert some 30,000 years ago. The civilization and techniques which made the explosion possible were wiped out. The only survivors were slaves marginal to the area who had no knowledge of its science or techniques. They became albinos as a result of radiation and scattered in different directions. Some of them went into Persia northern India Greece and Turkey. Others moved westward and settled in the caves of Europe. The descendants of the cave-dwelling albinos are the present inhabitants of America and western Europe. In these caves the white settlers contracted a virus passed down along their cursed generation that was to make them what they are today a hideous threat to life on this planet. This virus this ancient parasite is what Freud calls the unconscious spawned in the caves of Europe on flesh already diseased from radiation. Anyone descended from this line is basically different from those who have not had the cave experience and contracted this deadly sickness that lives in your blood and bones and nerves that lives where you used to live before your ancestors crawled into their filthy caves. When they came out of the caves they couldn't mind their own business. They had no business of their own to mind because they didn't belong to themselves any more. They belonged to the virus. They had to kill torture conquer enslave degrade as a mad dog has to bite. At Hiroshima all was lost. The metal sickness dormant 30,000 years stirring now in the blood and bones and bleached flesh. He cut himself shaving looked around for styptic pencil couldn't find one dabbed at his face with a towel remembering the smell and taste of burning metal in the tarnished mirror a teen-aged face crisscrossed with scar tissue pale grey eyes that seemed to be looking at something far away and long ago white white white as far as the eye can see ahead a blinding flash of white the cabin reeks of exploded star white lies the long denial from Christ to Hiroshima white voices always denying excusing the endless white papers why we dropped the atom bomb on Hiroshima how colonial peoples have benefited from our rule why look at all those schools and hospitals overgrown with weeds and vines windows melted dead hand frayed scar tissue lifted on a windy street lying white voices from the Congo to Newark the ancient mineral lie bleached flesh false human voices slow poison of rotting metal lies denials white papers *The Warren Report* he picked up a shirt white wash flapping in the cold spring wind Oppenheimer wipes a tear from one eye with one long finger.

"If it will shorten the war and save white lives . . ." (Difficult decision in the Pentagon).

Geologic strata of rotten lies and the vulgar strident affirmation "What are we waiting for? Let's bomb China now."

Nigger killing sheriff chuckling over the notches in his gun the old blind sheriff in his rocking chair.

"Bring me my gun son I wants to feel it."

"Yes father."

This was a ritual between them. Reverently the boy brought the old Colt .44 and put it in his father's twisted arthritic hands knarled fingers feeling the braille of notches and remembering . . . Remember the Congo? 15,000,000 blacks were systematically slaughtered by white bounty hunters. At first they were paid on presentation of a matched pair of ears. However some soft-hearted white hunters were just cutting off the ears and not doing the job like

"Now look black boy I got nothing against you just a job is all wife and kids back in England I'm a nice guy really. Now suppose I just cut off your ears and let you live naturally expect a little something for my trouble. How does that strike you?" "You sure is a good man, boss. You sure is a fair white man." However the fraud came to light and after that the bounty hunters were required to produce severed genitals as

95556

LIBRARY

College of St. Francis

JOLIET, ILL.

proof of performance. It is reported that some favored house niggers were allowed to remain as living eunuchs and that their gratitude was indescribable.

The foreman sits at a long table as the white hunters check in emptying the day's work on the table.

"You know I'm going to hang on to this bag. Give me birds a whiff of it."

Kerosene light his smile through cigarette smoke the foreman counts the genitals and sweeps them into a laundry hamper. He reaches into a drawer and counts out the money.

"There you are Scotty. Good English sterling."

"We're not mercenaries we're missionaries. My motto is 'send a kaffir a day to heaven.' "

"They are just black baboons."

"Just wave a welfare check over the river and them niggers will surface."

"Pass me some of that Redman" said the sheriff.

The officer said "I've been wanting to kill me a nigger for a long time."

"How long sir?"

The victims were Aubrey Pollard 19, Carl Cooper 17, and Fred Temple 18.

"Let's take care of Castro next and let's stay armed to the teeth for years decades centuries."

The Detroit police confirmed that they are investigating the three deaths at the Algiers motel. A riot commission is being set up. Welfare workers are asking questions in their whiney high-pitched voices. An old Jew retires to Miami Beach on fire insurance.

Ugly snarl behind the white lies and excuses. Look

at an ugly diseased white face. Look at the smoking mirror. Death rains back a hail of crystal skulls.

DEATH DEATH DEATH

Go out and get the pictures. Get all the pictures of

DEATH DEATH DEATH

For Citizen Kane who didn't like to hear the word spoken in his presence

DEATH DEATH DEATH

So many you can't remember
The boy who used to whistle?
Car accident or was it the war?
Which war?

The boy's room is quite empty now. Do you begin to see there is no face there in the tarnished mirror?

MY FACE

Let me say at the outset that I have for many years
been concerned with the possibility of taking over a
young body I would wake up stretch and look in the
mirror the lookout different just enough of the other
thoughts and feelings left to make it really new you
understand a dream old and banal as the fountain of
youth so on this day I left the house on Ladue Road.
After the death of my father the grounds have gone
down and the garden is overgrown with weeds. On
this day I walked out and was not particularly surprised to find things changed as if a new landscape had
been substituted for the old like a film backdrop. Walking at random I came around three in the afternoon to
an inn of sorts something between an English pub and
a company cafeteria. There was a small bar with
fireplace but the dining room was like a barn with zinc-
topped tables. This room was almost empty here and
there a few people drinking tea and reading newspapers. However the tables were all set as if many
more were expected. I sat down and noticed that the
sugar was grey and the tableware had the greasy black
feel common to jails, orphanages, mental hospitals or

other institution canteens. There was only one waiter and he immediately engaged my attention. He was about 19 years old with thin red hands and wrists. His face was splashed with red and his hair was sandy. He must be called Pinkie I decided. He showed me a menu on white paper splashed with gravy and I ordered roast lamb and mashed potatoes. It was as I recall quite tasteless. After the meal I called him to the table and with an assurance unknown to me ordinarily asked if he would be interested to aid me in an experiment he would be paid of course in any case he could decide for himself after we had discussed the details and where could we be private for a few minutes after he had finished work. He said that he was finished now and we could talk in his room. He led the way up stairs with worn red carpeting and brass strips. Room 18 on the top floor. Bleakly clear in the afternoon light an unmade bed, tarnished mirror over a washstand, a hot plate, a cup half-full of cold coffee in which floated the remains of a cigarette butt. He motioned me to a chair sat down on the bed and pulled a package of cigarettes from his shirt pocket. He lit one for himself and blew out the smoke.

"All right. Let's have it."

I explained that as soon as I saw him I had realized he was the person I was supposed to meet the one who could help me in an experiment of transference which would be of benefit to both of us perhaps of incalculable benefit but in all fairness not without danger.

"You mean we change places like?"

"Something like that . . ."

"Well what's the pay-off?"

I told him that I was prepared to pay him an immediate retainer of one hundred dollars but that much larger sums would be involved in the event of success, perhaps incalculable sums. I handed him five twenty-dollar bills which he shoved into his pocket without comment.

One thinks of such operations as involving electrical apparatus from a Frankenstein film, unknown drugs, bizarre sexual practices. It was nothing like that. I knew what to do and the apparatus was in my head, a triangle of light the apex of which extended about three feet and fitted into his head precisely at the source point. I felt a click and shift of outlines. The waiter was lying on his back head on the grimy pillow. I took off his shoes and covered him with a pink blanket. I walked over to the mirror. My movements seemed to require almost no effort. I was looking at my face in the mirror my new face. It was not exactly Pinkie's face nor mine. In fact I would hesitate to say that it was a face at all. Only the eyes were noticeable and these had a curious droop not unlike the eyes of a drug addict except that there was power and purpose in them. I saw also a red tie that I had not been wearing. Out on the stairs I hardly felt the worn carpet under my feet. The restaurant was deserted. I stepped in and suddenly the plates on the nearest table were whipped away as if by a great wind and crashed against the opposite wall. For a moment the Chinese cook appeared in the doorway. He looked at me, said one word in Chinese and closed the door. Again. As I proceeded through the restaurant crockery and silverware was swept from the tables on both sides of my path. I opened the side door and stepped out into a cobblestone alley. The day had been clear when I arrived at the inn. Now there were a few clouds in the sky. I had not reached the main road before the clouds had gathered and the sky darkened. As I stepped out of the alley rain fell in torrents. I don't know how long I walked around in the rain. Later much later I was looking into the mirror again rain dripping from my coat. I could see only the red tie and the drooping eyes. I turned toward the bed. Pinkie was still there under the blanket. I walked over and looked at him. I pulled the blanket back and felt a sudden pang in the heart and a prickling sensation at the back of my neck. He was thinner much thinner the ribs clearly visible under his open shirt. He opened his eyes and sat up. Then he said two words which I cannot bring myself to repeat. Later we were outside in the road. He was silent now and sullen.

"I will see you soon" I said.

He just nodded looking down at the cobblestones. Walking with difficulty stumbling on the stairs I found my way back to the room. When I woke up it was four in the afternoon. You understand his room chair by the bed three cigarettes in a shirt pocket garden outside in the afternoon light. I splashed some water on my face my new face and went downstairs. Standing in the stuffy little bar were two well-dressed men. They called me over.

"I am Lord Bothby and this is Doctor Harrison." We shook hands. "We would like to talk to you for a few minutes."

I said "All right" without enthusiasm. We sat down

at a table by the cold fireplace. The two men ordered Scotch and I had a pint of bitters.

"I will come straight to the point" said Lord Bothby "You see we know who you are."

"In that case you know more than I do."

"Exactly. You need our help."

"To do what exactly?"

"You may not realize the importance of the discovery you have made the uh success of your preliminary experiment. It is in your power to shape the entire future of this planet."

"Does it have a future?"

"That will depend on you . . . whether you are willing to accept expert guidance and do what is necessary. You must be prepared to lay aside all preconceptions of a sentimental nature."

In a flash I saw the emaciated body of the waiter under a torn pink blanket and realized that as the "experiments" continued the body would be always more drained. And then?

As if anticipating my thought Lord Bothby said "When the present subject is no longer serviceable we will know where to find another. The power must be guided."

I almost said "If you know so much more than I do why do you need me?" However I had already perceived that Lord Bothby and Doctor Harrison were nothing but film extras and I might see his lordship a few days from now behind the bar of some pub and the learned doctor driving a hack. Looking past them I glimpsed a far flung organization with unlimited funds and well-trained ruthless agents. I would do well to exercise caution. I thanked them for their interest and promised to consider carefully what they had told me and to meet them here on Friday afternoon. Afterward I took my leave and went to the kitchen where I told the Chinese cook I would be taking the day off. He just nodded without looking around. I knew I would find Pinkie in my house on Ladue Road. He was sitting in the downstairs living room reading a science-fiction magazine. He greeted me apathetically. I had hoped he would prove an ally against the two agents and the organization they represented. In this I was disappointed. He listened to my account without interest shrugged and lit a cigarette. A wave of depression and horror swept over me.

"Look Pinkie I don't want to go on with this. There must be a way back. I'd be willing to reverse roles anything you like."

"I don't know anything about it" he said sullenly. "It was your idea not mine." After a meal of tinned beans and tea we went to the upstairs bedroom where my father died and made love. I remember it was dim and sad like making love to an empty body. Looking up at the dark ceiling lit occasionally by the headlights of passing cars phrases in my mind flat trite phrases from some old science-fiction magazine. "They called me. Doctor Harrison." Shook hands without enthusiasm looked sullenly at the floor turned abruptly away lighting a cigarette far flung organization ruthless agents unlimited funds you may not realize the importance of the Chinese preliminary experiments greeted me without interest in the gathering shadows incalculable sums the grimy pillow I took my leave. The last

word is written lost voice whispering in the living
room that night of stale cigarette smoke a moment
palpable in the air years later I remember London the
grimy stations and the tracks your name remains as
the human structure not a word is mine I have no
words left breathing old pulp magazines in the living
dust of the dead Gods lonely fringes of a remote gal-
axy a million light-years away the pale skies fall apart
T.B. waiting at the next stop spit blood at dawn is it
later I remember London grimy pants open I pulled at
my face in the mirror my new face agony to remember the words "Too Late." Don't you understand
overgrown with weeds a long time. Do you begin to
see there is no face there in the tarnished mirror? I was
waiting there pale character in someone else's writing
they called me years later your name remains breathing in these trite phrases. T.B. waiting at the next stop
pale emaciated body of the waiter. Remember the boy
who used to whistle? bleakly clear the suburban gardens mirror over a cheap chest of drawers. I was waiting there. "They called me. Doctor Harrison." Led
the way up. Head on a grimy pillow phantom voice
whispering in the living room. "Too late." Agony to
remember the old human structure dim buildings overgrown with vines.

I remember a room where the lights wouldn't turn
on and later in Mexico City I see myself on a street
looking at him as if trying to focus to remember who
the stranger was standing under a dusty tree thin
boy ruffled brown hair light blue eyes blank factual
I remember London grimy pants open stairs worn
red carpeting the smell of oranges and I could see

his pants were sticking up between his legs far pale sun the wind ruffled brown hair a colored photograph and something written . . . *"Vuelvete y aganchete"* . . . I let myself go limp inside blank factual he slid it in out through the little dusty window pale light over worn-out hills the old broken point of origin St Louis Missouri smell of sickness in the room head on the grimy pillow a million light-years away there was nothing for me to do his head on a pillow spit blood at dawn.

"They called me. Doctor Harrison."

Remember what hope feels like I was sitting by the bed the last words face very pale breathing into the mirror . . .

Then he said something: your name

Pulled the blanket up: my face

And there he is again walking around some day later across the street smiled round the corner so long ago the old grey corner blurred sadness in his eyes the corner shop I was walking behind him at the corner said something . . . one word . . . no dice flickered across his good bye his mouth a little open there looking for a name it is getting dark boy burglar spots the door open.

"Abrupt question brought me Mister."

Desolate thin blue overcoat far to go a street sadness in his eyes looking for a name . . .

Click of distant heels . . .

WIND DIE. YOU DIE. WE DIE.

Under a dim moon and dim stars I walked down to a clearing over the sea where I had made love to a girl some night before. She could not have known that her romantic middle-aged lover was actually a stranded pederast who had experienced considerable strain in fulfilling his male role. Anything is better than nothing is a very bad approach to sex. I stood there hearing the sound of the sea several hundred feet down at the bottom of a steep slope, feeling the wind on my face and remembering the wind on our bodies, the wind that is life to Puerto de los Santos. *Los vientos de Dios,* the winds of God that blow away the mosquitoes and the miasmal mists and the swamp smells. The winds of God that keep the great hairy tarantulas and the poisonous snakes at bay. The natives have a saying: "Wind die. You die. We die." I knew that this could happen. In fact I had written a thesis showing that low-pressure areas were shifting inexorably to the east and that the winds of God must soon die. My thesis had not been well received by the local officials who were preoccupied with the possibility of a modern airport and jet service from Miami. Soon they told each other

American tourists loaded with money would come to enjoy the winds of God, the dry balmy wind like a great fan from the sea that kept the temperature just right day and night the year round.

"If only we had some Communists to fight" said the officials sadly. "Then we could be sure the Americans would give us money."

Somewhere in the distance a dog was barking from a villa garden. I turned and walked back to the empty sea road under the dim moon and dim stars.

The lack of Communists it seems was crucial and the airline made arrangements elsewhere. Then an ominous portent of disaster touched Puerto de los Santos. The winds of God were dying. Today whole sections of the foreign quarter are deserted. The swimming pools are full of stagnant rainwater. In the desolate markets the bright fabrics and tinware no longer flap and clatter in the winds of God. There are few purchasers and fingers that touch the merchandise are yellow and listless with fever. The mosquitoes have returned and the swamp smells, the great hairy tarantulas and the poisonous snakes. Puerto de los Santos is dying.

In my New York apartment I remember that spot over the sea. No lovers would go there now because of the mosquitoes the spiders and the snakes. It is getting dark and I stand by the window looking at the lights of New York. This city will also die. Remember the power failure some years ago? It was never explained to anyone's satisfaction least of all to mine. In fact I have written a thesis to show that, owing to reverse magnetic currents, there will soon be no electricity conducted on the Eastern seaboard. My thesis has been shelved in Washington. People do not like to hear these things. I know that in a few years the Great White Way will black out forever. I can see darkness falling in great blocks on the stricken town. Before that happens I will be somewhere else no doubt writing another thesis that will not be well received by the local officials. I stand at the window and remember the wind on our bodies the sound of the sea dim jerky far away stars . . .

"Wind die. You die. We die."

THE END.

I turned the page to be faced by a lurid color picture of a creature with pendulous leathery breasts, two front legs ending in claws and a scorpion's tail. They had the breasts of women, a scorpion's sting and snapping teeth! They came in countless hordes and they attacked!

The Crawling Breasts

Tommy Wentworth, an assistant baker, was riding home on his bicycle after work. He lived a few miles out of town and rode to and from work every day. As he passed St Hill he heard a curious sound like the clacking of many castanets. He stopped and leaned his bicycle against a tree. St Hill, so named for a local saint who had killed a dragon, was covered with trees, vines and heavy undergrowth. On weekends Tommy often came here with his friends to pick berries. He heard the sound again louder now. What could it be? And the sound of many bodies slithering through the underbrush. Why it sounded like an army. He walked a little way up the hill and pushed aside the brush. A few minutes later he was panting out his story to a skeptical constable.

"Women you say now with hanging breasts walking on two front legs? Scorpion stings and snapping teeth is it? You wouldn't have been stopping in at the Swan for a few pints would you now?" The constable winked broadly.

"But I tell you I saw them! And coming this way!"

The constable looked up sharply. Colonel Sutton-Smith was standing in the doorway a sporting rifle under his arm.

"Constable there are some sort of monsters advancing on the village. We must call up every able-bodied man between the ages of fourteen and seventy with whatever weapons they can lay hand to. Have them assemble at St Hill Green."

The constable turned pale. "*Monsters* you say sir? You *saw* them sir?"

"Yes through my binoculars. They will reach the village in a quarter hour more or less. There is no time to waste."

The constable opened a drawer and took out an old Bulldog Webley .455. He looked at it dubiously.

"I doubt if it will fire sir after all these years . . . must be some cartridges about somewheres."

The colonel turned to Tommy. "And now my boy get on your bicycle and cover the houses on the east side of the road down to Shelby's Farm. Tell the men to collect whatever weapons they can find and report to the Green. Women and children to stay locked in the houses. The constable and I will cover the west side. Look sharp now."

Ten minutes later thirty frightened men and boys stood on the Green armed with shotguns, pickaxes, iron bars, meat cleavers and cobblestones. Lanterns had been lit casting an orange glow over Dragon Lake. Buckets of petrol stood ready to burn the monsters.

"Here they come!" Tommy shouted.

"Form a square men" the colonel snapped. He raised his rifle.

"Mr Anderson will see you now. Will you kindly step this way Mr Seward." Somewhat reluctantly I put down the magazine and followed her down a long corridor. Funny what you find in old pulp magazines. "Wind die. We die. You die." Quite haunting actually . . . the middle-aged Tiresias moving from place to place with his unpopular thesis, spending his days in public libraries, eking out a living writing fiction for pulp magazines . . . good stories too . . . the dim night sky the place by the sea the shadowy figure of the absent girl . . . you can see it all somehow . . . Curiously enough I had myself come to sound a word of warning, a warning I was reasonably sure would not be heeded. Still a man has his duty. And I was reluctant to leave the intrepid colonel frozen forever rifle at his shoulder. Perhaps I could pinch the magazine on the way out. I doubted this. The receptionist had a sharp cold eye. She opened a door.

Mr Anderson was crisp and cool. "And what can I do for you Mr Seward."

"Mr Anderson I wonder if you have read my treatise on the possibility of virus replication *outside* the host cell?"

Mr Anderson looked at once vague and desperate. "Well no I can't say that I have."

"The treatise is theoretical of course. I have not come here to discuss theories Mr Anderson. I have come to warn you that virus replication *outside* the host cell is now an accomplished fact. Unless the most drastic measures are taken *at once* . . . measures so drastic I hesitate to tell you what they are . . . unless these measures are taken Mr Anderson within two years or less the entire male population of this district will be reduced to—"

"Mr Capwell will see you now Mr Bently. Will you step this way please." Somewhat reluctantly I put down the magazine and followed her down the hall. Quite an idea. Story of someone reading a story of someone reading a story. I had the odd sensation that I myself would wind up in the story and that someone would read about me reading the story in a waiting room somewhere. As I followed her down the corridor the words I had read began shifting in my head all their own as it were . . . shifting inexorably to a spot over the sea . . . the distance a dog was barking from . . . this spot . . . deserted swimming pool at the bottom of a steep slope . . . villa garden . . . bright wind in the desolate markets . . . our bodies reflected . . . tinware clattering in the winds of God . . . Swan for a few pints would you now? I turned the page to be faced by his leathery breasts . . . Two Claws Smith was standing in the doorway . . . She could not know that her stranded pederast had experienced arrangements elsewhere . . . louder now the sound of something out forever . . . Exactly what would the male population of the district be reduced to and what were the "drastic measures" by which Mr Seward proposed to avert such reduction? Perhaps I could charm the magazine out of the receptionist. I nearly laughed aloud at the thought that I might wind up making love to her under a dim night sky in a clearing over the sea. She turned and flashed me a smile as she opened a door. It was a smile that said "I wish you luck. He's a real bastard." He was indeed. He looked at me as if he were trying to focus my face through a telescope.

"Yes Mr uh Bently." Clearly he suspected me of using an assumed name. "And what can I do for you?"

"Mr uh Capwell what can you do for your own reflection many times removed of course or to put it another way on the subject of wrongness how wrong do you think you generally are?"

He visibly experienced more difficulty in focusing my face.

"I don't believe I understand you Mr Bently."

"In that case I will make yourself clearer. But first let me ask if you have entertained certain elementary considerations with regard to repetitive irritations of virus origin? One sneeze for example is inconsequential whereas a thousand consecutive sneezes might well prove fatal . . . the common cold Mr Capwell uncommon to be sure in this climate and for that very reason should you leave Panama and return to New York it is your duty to know and mine to inform you that you would have as it were an unseen traveler's companion

of the most regrettable and I may add versatile pro-
clivities. No Mr Capwell this is not a Communist plot.
It is simply the mirror image of such a plot many
times removed and apparent to you as such because
you believe that it is. You know of course that it is a
common measure of prophylaxis to shoot a cow with
the aftosa and that a reasonable cow would not object
to this procedure if that cow had been indoctrinated
with the proper feelings of duty toward the bovine
community at large. Does that answer your question
Mr Capwell?"

When you look down a snub-nosed .38 you can see
the bullet at the bottom of the barrel. It gives you a
funny feeling many times removed.

"You can see Miss Blankslip now Mr Tomlinson."

"In focusing my face Thompson is the name."

"Oh yes Mr Thompson if you'll just care to step this
way . . . It is in the East wing . . . I'll see you past
the guards."

"Did I understand you to say Miss Blankslip?"

"Yes she has remained unmarried" the boy told me.
"It is said that she experienced a great disappoint-
ment in love many years ago but that was in another
country and besides her present condition would make
matrimony an interesting but remote contingency."

We were walking through what appeared to be an
abandoned compound or concentration camp . . .
rusty barbed wire, concrete ditches and barriers overgrown with weeds and vines. Here and there the concrete was blackened by some fire long ago. We passed
three barriers where a guard lounged, tunic unbut-

toned, rusty revolver in holster green with mold. They waved us through with listless yellow fingers. A sour rotten smell of stale flesh and sweat hung over the compound like a smog.

"The odor of course is still here. You see there has been no wind since . . ." It was getting dark. I had a curious feeling of being three feet back of my head. Years ago I had studied something called Scientology I believe. As if seen through a telescope from a great distance I read the following words: "In other words, two of each of anything, one facing the other. By bracket we mean, of course, putting them up as himself as though they were put up by somebody else, the somebody else facing the somebody else, and the matched terminal again put up by others facing others." Mirror images mocked up opposite each other each pair placed there by the next in line. We had reached the edge of a brown lake lit by carbide lanterns. In the shallow water I could see crablike fish that stirred the surface occasionally releasing bubbles of stagnant swamp smell. A few trees grew here of a strangely bulbous and distorted variety. Gathered in this desolate spot were a handful of ragged soldiers diseased and dirty. One of them stepped forward and handed me an old Webley .455. An officer with a rusty sporting rifle under his arm returned my salute. We were standing in front of what appeared to be an abandoned barracks. The receptionist turned to us with the manner of a circus barker.

"And now folks if you'll just step this way you are about to witness the most amazing the most astounding living monstrosity of all time. She was once a beautiful woman.''

He unlocked the door and we filed in. A terrible unknown stench seared the lungs and grabbed the stomach. Several soldiers retched into faded bandanas. In the center of the dusty room was a wire mesh cubicle where something stirred sluggishly. I felt an overwhelming nightmare vertigo.

"You! You! You!"

It was the end of the line.

END OF THE LINE

When Agent W.E.9 returned from London he found
his quarters bugged, his assistant and technician I.S.
on the verge of collapse, owing to continual insults and
harassments in the street. Clearly enemy agents had
been busy during his absence. W.E.9 analyzed the situation. Since the harassment was coming from Arab
subjects, he must look for someone who spoke and
wrote Arabic. Now since all events are written he must
also find a *writer*. The most obvious subject was of
course Mr P. who was a writer. In fact the particular
form of the harassments bore his style his mark. The
Arabs called I.S. the "Mad Woman." He was jeered
at in the streets and very near just such a complete
breakdown as *westerners in contact with Arabs ha-
bitually undergo in the novels of Mr P.* However Mr
P. spoke Arabic but did not write it. W.E.9 must find
an agent who wrote Arabic, who also knew English,
and would be capable of translating Mr P.'s continuity
into Arabic characters, and passing along through chan-
nels. In order to achieve results of course pictures
would also be necessary. However, many photos of I.S.
and of the house at 4 Calle Larachi were already in
enemy hands. Now a writer who simply transcribes

into another language continuity written or taped—in this case undoubtedly taped in Arabic—into another language is known as a "Blind Writer" in the trade. W.E.9's first step was to find the "Blind Writer." These agents are always camouflaged. "Look for someone you have never thought of as a friend or an enemy" the D.S. always said "or to put it another way if you wish to hide anything it is simply necessary to create disinterest in the area where it is hidden. Look for someone who arouses in you no feeling but disinterest."

W.E.9 found the "Blind Writer" there by the Dutch Bank where Martin's book shop used to be. The man he looked for had just left the Dutch Bank and was walking south: Old Doctor Bronquites. Click: memory pictures coming in Socco Chico 1956, D.B. in his dirty white linen suit his dirty white beard stained yellow with cheap cigarettes shabby and inconspicuous behind dark glasses—yes he *looked* blind, and old and evil his presence anywhere taking away vitality and light. W.E.9 remembered the only joke he ever heard the good doctor tell. It was just after the nationalization of the Suez Canal. "Arab standing by the canal with his dirty pictures. Feelthier than ever." D.B. Dirty Books hum . . . W.E.9 stepped out of the book shop barring the doctor's path—without the dark glasses now—W.E.9 looked straight into the hideous insect evil of Minraud. He held out his hand.

"Doctor Bronquites."

The doctor looked at him blankly and then

"Ah W.B., but what has happened to you? Have you been ill?"

"You're looking good yourself doctor."

"Ah no, heart trouble you know."

The doctor got into an open car with a young couple and drove away.

"Heart trouble—yes . . . hum . . . new suit . . . just coming out of the Dutch Bank—been paid off for something—click 1956 Socco Chico—the doctor there drinking one of the two cups of coffee his small pension from what country? For what services? allowed him per day. D.B. was Dutch, he had lived 40 years in Egypt. Expelled under Nasser. Why? He claimed to be a medical doctor, and yet W.E.9, who had studied medicine six months in Vienna, knew more medicine than the doctor. One thing was certain. He spoke and wrote both Arabic and English. In fact gave lessons in Arabic to supplement his pension. (Parenthetically besides being W.E.9's photographer and technical assistant, I.S. was attempting to learn Arabic. W.E.9 could tick off a list of agents who had been murdered because they might learn to read and write Arabic— P.W. a young poet who learned Arabic in a matter of days—Addicted to heroin by J.S. Died 1956 in Paris . . . cause of death unknown . . . "The Paul did it— The Paul The Paul—The Paul" . . . A young student at Harvard 1936 who had mastered colloquial Egyptian Arabic . . . Drunk . . . slid downstairs and broke his neck—Ali was learning English . . . Died . . . prison hospital Ben Baroud, Tangier cause of death "He fell downstairs" you know the old cop bullshit . . .) W.E.9 decided to send a visitor to D.B. without delay. Heart trouble would make it easy.

The car carrying Doctor B. turned right on Mohammed V. The doctor was amazing his new friends by chanting the prayer call as it used to be done in Cairo and telling his few stories.

"Yes you will see a woman there of three hundred pounds so fat she can hardly walk and beside her a man so thin as a stick, and he is very proud."

"Oh isn't he marvelous?" said the girl. She rumpled the doctor's white hair. "I think he's cute don't you?"

"Yes he's cute all right."

The car was gathering speed on the road to Tetuán.

"But where are we going?" said the doctor. "I have to give an Arab lesson at two o'clock."

"You can cut a class can't you?" said the young man pressing harder on the accelerator. "We're all going to Tetuán or Chouen maybe."

"But this is impossible—I tell you—I must be at my hotel by two o'clock."

"Now doctor" the girl rumpled his hair—"A little change of air will do you no end of good."

"Stop the car! Let me out!" He looked wildly at the driver. The young man who an hour before when he first met them in the Café de Paris, had seemed such a harmless young tourist, wore a cold closed look. He pressed the accelerator to the floor without looking around. The car shot into a side road, skidded, the driver pulled out of the skid, expertly slowed down to fifty. The car pulled up in front of a deserted roadhouse the tattered awning flapping in the wind. It was the end of the line.

THE DRUMS OF DEATH

The coachman left him at the door of the villa and drove hastily away. He had wanted to ask about some-one to do the cleaning and prepare one meal a day but the man seemed in a hurry to be off. It was only three miles to the village. He could walk in and make inquiries the following day. The villa was in a clump of pine trees with a view over the lake. It seemed to be ideal for his purposes, a study on the second floor with a massive oak desk. He felt sure that he would be able to finish the novel he was working on. The end had given him trouble and he had come here in search of solitude. After a quick inspection of the rooms he walked down a path between pine trees to the lake. About three hundred yards from the shore was an is-land with weeping willows trailing in the water and pines on the summit. He thought of Rachmaninoff's "Isle of the Dead" . . . Perhaps this was the clue he needed. It was almost six o'clock and the sun had al-ready disappeared behind the mountains that encir-cled the lake. He stripped off his clothes on a sudden impulse. He would swim out to the island and have a look around. His canvas shoes he tied around his waist.

He waded into the water which was not as cold as he had expected. The bank fell steeply away to deep water. He swam with a feeling of great ease and freedom but it seemed a long time before he reached the island. There it was now just in front of him in the gathering twilight suddenly dark and foreboding. And he became aware of a sound or vibration like the beating of a drum. And then he looked up and perceived a long skinny shape outlined against the sky. A wave of sick horror swept over him and he was sinking down down into a sucking whirlpool. When he came to himself he was in the villa on a bed. The coachman and another man he had not seen before stood over him. The other man who was the village doctor gave him an injection and he fell into a deep sleep. He was delirious for a week and nearly died. Later as the story goes an enemy imitated the drumbeats and nearly drove him to madness. However, he found the drum and one night when this man came to his house Dahlfar stood in the shadows and beat the drum. The enemy went into a blind panic and jumped over a cliff into the sea. He who plays death must keep the drum. DEATH, O foolish Scribe, come and took over.

hillside over the sea. man sitting there on a cane seat
. . . he is dressed in old-fashioned puttees green sport
coat of English cut he has a sandy mustache stained
with tobacco pale blue eyes . . . near him we now see
several convulsed forms, the closest a few feet away
outstretched hand clutching a handful of grass . . .
the camera pans out convulsed corpses to the sky back
to the man sitting there on his cane seat . . . the man
takes a chicken sandwich out of a wicker lunch basket
. . . "safe at last" he says and starts eating his sandwich . . . the man you see here is Doctor Lee . . .
Doctor John Lee . . . he was a sensitive man and it
lacerated him to walk streets and enter restaurants
where he encountered living organisms manifesting
wills different from and in some cases flatly antagonis-
tic to his own . . . "the situation is little short of in-
tolerable" . . . Rock Ape waiter there with the wrong
wine . . . he was a timid man in a way you see and not
able to fix the waiter with Mandrill eyes and ugly
American snarl . . . "bring me *red* wine you hairy
assed Rock Ape or I drink it from your throat!" . . .
now the doctor was a man of independent means and

could usually avoid such disturbing incidents but the possibility was always there . . . this disturbed him and he was a man who did not like to be disturbed . . . he decided to end the whole distasteful thing once and for all by turning everyone into himself . . . this he proposed to do by a virus an image concentrate of himself that would spread waves of tranquillity in all directions until the world was a fit place for him to live . . . he called it the "beautiful disease" . . . his first attempts to activate the image meal failed . . . he realized of course that to administer a dead or weakened strain of the beautiful Lee virus would invite the disaster of mass inoculation . . . he had to be quite sure you understand . . . some of his "canine preparations" as he called test cases died in quite unpleasant ways that disturbed him for he was a humane man and did not like to be disturbed so these unworthy vessels only increased his resolve to make a better world . . . one day it occurred to him if perhaps the image meal were radioactive . . . he painted a culture of image meal with radium paint and put it in an iron box covered on the outside with layers of human skin and now he chuckled "let it steep" and made himself a cup of tea . . . he finished his tea and opened the box . . . "ladies and gentlemen of planet earth introducing 'Johnny 23' " . . . his cat hissed made an abortive attempt to walk on its hind legs and fell in convulsions . . . in its dying eyes he read an almost human hatred . . . he attributed the death of his cat to a short circuit of overburdened synapsis occasioned by a too rapid conversion to the human condition . . . "now we must find a worthy vessel" . . . remember the good doctor was a humane man who did not like to harm anyone because it disturbed him to do so and he was a man who did not like to be disturbed . . . he had convinced himself that "Johnny 23" would simply remove from the planet hostile alien forces manifesting themselves through other people that this would come about through peaceful penetration in the course of which no lives would be lost . . . "Johnny 23" would simply make friends of everyone . . . the doctor was not a man who argued with himself . . . the first public appearance of "Johnny 23" demonstrated a miscalculation . . . worthy vessels clutched at an often imaginary mustache and fell in convulsions looking at some invisible presence black hate from dying eyes . . . "Johnny 23" was one hundred percent fatal . . . the good doctor had a spot of bother a narrow escape in fact when the worthy vessels found out who "Johnny 23" is . . . fortunately the epidemic was well advanced by that time and "Johnny 23" finished the job . . . he finishes his sandwich and licks the grease off his fingers . . . he puts a cigarette in a stained bone holder . . . he sits there smoking . . . it is very peaceful there on the hillside nothing to disturb him as far as the eyes can see he gets up folds his cane seat and walks down a path toward the sea . . . his boat is moored by the pier . . . it is a small boat and he can handle it alone . . . last awning flaps on the pier . . . last man here now.

THE DISCIPLINE OF DE

A cold dry windy day clouds blowing through the sky sunshine and shadow. A dead leaf brushes my face. The streets remind me of St Louis . . . red brick houses, trees, vacant lots. Bright and windy back in a cab through empty streets. When I reach the fourth floor it looks completely unfamiliar as if seen through someone else's eyes.

"I hope you find your way . . . red brick houses, trees . . . the address in empty streets."

Colonel Sutton-Smith, 65, retired not uncomfortably on a supplementary private income . . . flat in Bury Street St James . . . cottage in Wales . . . could not resign himself to the discovery of Roman coins under the grounds of his cottage interesting theory the Colonel has about those coins over two sherries never a third no matter how nakedly his guest may leer at the adamant decanter. He can of course complete his memoirs . . . extensive notes over a period of years, invitations, newspaper clippings, photographs, stretching into the past on yellowing dates. Objects go with the clippings, the notes, the photos, the dates . . . A kris on the wall to remember Ali who ran amok in the marketplace of Lampipur thirty years ago, a crown of emerald quartz, a jade head representing a reptilian youth with opal eyes, a little white horse delicately carved in ivory, a Webley .455 automatic revolver . . . (Only automatic revolver ever made the cylinder turns on ratchets stabilizing like a gyroscope the heavy recoil.) Memories, objects stuck in an old calendar. The Colonel decides to make his own time. He opens a school notebook with lined papers and constructs a simple calendar consisting of ten months with 26 days in each month to begin on this day February 21, 1970, Raton Pass 14 in the new calendar. The months have names like old Pullman cars in America where the Colonel had lived until his 18th year . . . names like Beauacres, Bonneterre, Watford Junction, Sioux Falls, Pikes Peak, Yellowstone, Bellevue, Cold Springs, Lands End dated from the beginning Raton Pass 14 a mild grey day. Smell of soot and steam and iron and cigar smoke as the train jolts away into the past. The train is stopped now red brick buildings a deep blue canal outside the train window a mild grey day long ago. The Colonel is jolted back to THE NOW by a plate streaked with egg yolk, a bacon rind, toast crumbs on the table, a jumble of morning papers, cigarette butt floating in cold coffee right where you are sitting now. The Colonel decides, on this mild grey day, to bring his time into present time. He looks at the objects on the breakfast table calculating the moves to clear it. He measures the distance of his chair to the table how to push chair back and stand up without hitting the table with his legs. He pushes chair back and stands up. With smooth precise movements he scrapes his plate into The Business News of *The Times*, folds the paper into a neat triangular packet, sweeps up plate, knife, fork, spoon and coffee cup out to the kitchen with no fumbling or wasted movements washed and put away. Before he made the first move he has planned a whole series of moves ahead. He has discovered the simple and basic Discipline of DE. DO EASY. It is simply to do everything you do in the *easiest* and most relaxed manner you can achieve at the time you do it. He becomes an assiduous student of DE. Cleaning the flat is a problem in logistics. He knows every paper every object and many of them now have names. He has perfected the art of "casting" sheets and blankets so they fall just so. And the gentle silent spoon or cup on a table . . . He practices for a year before he is ready to reveal the mysteries of DE . . .

As the Colonel washes up and tidies his small kitchen the television audience catches its breath in front of the little screen. Knives forks and spoons flash through his fingers and tinkle into drawers. Plates dance onto the shelf. He touches the water taps with gentle precise fingers and just enough pressure considering the rubber washers inside. Towels fold themselves and fall softly into place. As he moves he tosses crumpled papers and empty cigarette packages over his shoulder and under his arms and they land unerringly in the wastebasket as a Zen master can hit the target with his arrow in the dark. He moves through the sitting room a puff of air from his cupped hand delicately lifts a cigarette ash from the table and wafts it into a wastebasket. Into the bedroom smooth movements cleaning the sink and arranging the toilet articles into a *nature morte* different each day. With one fluid rippling cast the sheets crinkle into place and the blankets follow tucked· in with fingers that feel the cloth and mattress. In two minutes the flat is dazzling . . .

The Colonel Issues Beginners DE

DE is a way of *doing*. It is a way of doing everything you do. DE simply means doing whatever you do in the *easiest* most relaxed way you can manage which is also the quickest and most efficient way as you will find as you advance in DE.

You can start right now tidying up your flat, moving furniture or books, washing dishes, making tea, sorting papers. Consider the weight of objects exactly how much force is needed to get the object from here to there. Consider its shape and texture and function where exactly does it belong. Use just the amount of force necessary to get the object from here to there. Don't fumble jerk grab an object. Drop cool possessive fingers onto it like a gentle old cop making a soft arrest. Guide a dustpan lightly to the floor as if you were landing a plane. When you touch an object weigh it with your fingers feel your fingers on the object the skin blood muscles tendons of your hand and arm. Consider these extensions of yourself as precision instruments to perform every movement smoothly and well. Handle objects with consideration and they will show you all their little tricks. Don't tug or pull at a zipper. Guide the little metal teeth smoothly along feeling the sinuous ripples of cloth and flexible metal. Replacing the cap on a tube of tooth paste . . . (and this should always be done at once few things are worse than an uncapped tube maladroitly squeezed twisting up out of the bathroom glass drooling paste unless it be a tube with the cap barbarously forced on all askew against the threads). Replacing the cap let the very tips of your fingers protrude beyond the cap contacting the end of the tube guiding the cap into place. Using your finger tips as a landing gear will enable you to drop any light object silently and surely into its place. Remember every object has its place. If you don't find that place and put that thing there it will jump out at you and trip you or rap you painfully across the knuckles. It will nudge you and clutch at you and get in your way. Often such objects belong in the wastebasket but often it's just that they are out of place. Learn to place an object firmly and quietly in its place and do not let your fingers move that object as they leave it there. When you put down a cup separate your fingers cleanly from the cup. Do not let them catch in the handle and if they do repeat movement until fingers separate clean. If you don't catch that nervous finger that won't let go of that handle you may twitch hot tea across the Duchess. Never let a poorly executed sequence pass. If you throw a match at a wastebasket and miss get right up and put that match in the wastebasket. If you have time repeat the cast that failed. There is always a reason for missing an easy toss. Repeat toss and you will find it. If you rap your knuckles against a window jamb or door, if you brush your leg against a desk or a bed, if you catch your feet in the curled-up corner of a rug, or strike a toe against a desk or chair go back and repeat the sequence. You will be surprised to find how far off course you were to hit that window jamb that door that chair. Get back on course and do it again. How can you pilot a spacecraft if you can't find your way around your own apartment? It's just like retaking a movie shot until you get it right. And you will begin to feel yourself in a film moving with ease and speed. But don't try for speed at first. Try for relaxed smoothness taking as much time as you need to perform action. If you drop an object, break an object, spill anything, knock painfully against anything, galvanically clutch an object pay particular attention to retake. You may find out why and forestall a repeat performance. If the object is broken sweep up pieces and remove from the room at once. If object is intact or you have duplicate object repeat sequence. You may experience a strange feeling as if the objects are alive and hostile trying to twist out of your fingers, slam noisily down on a table, jump out at you and stub your toe or trip you. Repeat sequence until objects are brought to order.

Here is student at work. At two feet he tosses red plastic milk cap at the orange garbage bucket. The cap sails over the bucket like a flying saucer. He tries again. Same result. He examines the cap and finds that one edge is crushed down. He pries the edge back into place. Now the cap will drop obediently into the bucket. Every object you touch is alive with your life and your will.

The student tosses cigarette box at wastebasket and it bounces out from the cardboard cover from a metal coat hanger which is resting diagonally across the wastebasket and never should be there at all. If an ash tray is emptied into that wastebasket the cardboard triangle will split the ashes and the butts scattering both on the floor. Student takes a box of matches from his coat pocket preparatory to lighting cigarette from new package on table. With the matches in one hand he makes another toss and misses of course his fingers are in future time lighting a cigarette. He retrieves package puts the matches down and now stopping slightly legs bent hop skip over the washstand and into the wastebasket, miracle of the Zen master who hits a target in the dark these little miracles will occur more and more often as you advance in DE . . . the ball of paper tossed over a shoulder into the wastebasket, the blanket flipped and settled just into place that seems to fold itself under the brown satin fingers of an old Persian merchant. Objects move into place at your lightest touch. You slip into it like a film moving with such ease you hardly know you are doing it. You'd come into the kitchen expecting to find a sink full of dirty dishes and instead every dish is put away and the kitchen shines. The Little People have been there and done your work fingers light and cold as spring wind through the rooms.

The student considers heavy objects. Tape recorder on the desk taking up too much space and he doesn't use it very often. So put it under the washstand. Weigh it with the hands. First attempt the cord and socket leaps across the desk like a frightened snake. He bumps his back on the washstand putting the recorder under it. Try again lift with legs not back. He hits the lamp. He looks at that lamp. It is a horrible disjointed object the joints tightened with cellophane tape disconnected when not in use the cord leaps out and wraps around his feet sometimes jerking the lamp off the desk. Remove that lamp from the room and buy a new one. Now try again lifting shifting pivoting dropping on the legs just so and right under the washstand.

You will discover clumsy things you've been doing for years until you think that is just the way things are. Here is an American student who for years has clawed at the red plastic cap on English milk bottle you see American caps have a little tab and he has been looking for that old tab all these years. Then one day in a friend's kitchen he saw a cap depressed at the center. Next morning he tries it and the miracle occurs. Just the right pressure in the center and he lifts the cap off with deft fingers and replaces it. He does this several times in wonder and in awe and well he might him a college professor and very technical too planarium worms learn quicker than that for years he has been putting on his socks after he puts on his pants so he has to roll up pants and pants and socks get clawed in together so why not put on the socks *before* the pants? He is learning the simple miracles . . . The Miracle of the Washstand Glass . . . we all know the glass there on a rusty razor blade streaked with pink tooth paste a decapitated tube writhing up out of it . . . quick fingers go to work and the Glass sparkles like The Holy Grail in morning sunlight. Now he does a wallet drill. For years he has carried his money in the left side pocket of his pants reaching down to fish out the naked money . . . bumping his fingers against the sharp edges of notes. Often the notes were in two stacks and pulling out the one could drop the other on the floor. The left side pocket of the pants is most difficult to pick but worse things can happen than a picked pocket one can dine out on that for a season. Two manicured fingers sliding into the well-cut suit wafted into the waiting hand an engraved message from the Queen. Surely this is the easy way. Besides no student of DE would have his pocket picked applying DE in the street, picking his route through slower walkers, don't get stuck behind that baby carriage, *careful* when you round a corner don't bump into somebody coming round the other way. He takes the wallet out in front of a mirror, removes notes, counts notes, replaces notes. as rapidly as he can with no fumbling, catching note edges on wallet, or other errors. That is a basic principle which must be repeated. When speed is crucial to the operation you must find your speed the fastest you can perform the operation without error. Don't try for speed at first it will come his fingers will rustle through the wallet with a touch light as dead leaves and crinkle discreetly the note that will bribe a South American customs official into overlooking a shrunk-down head. The customs agent smiles a collector's smile the smile of a connoisseur. Such a crinkle he has not heard since a French jewel thief with crudely forged papers made a crinkling sound over them with his hands and there is the note neatly folded into a false passport.

Now some one will say . . . "But if I have to *think* about every move I make" . . . You only have to think and break down movement into a series of still pictures to be studied and corrected because you have not found the easy way. Once you find the easy way you don't have to think about it It will almost do itself.

Operations performed on your person . . . brushing teeth, washing, etc. can lead you to correct a defect before it develops. Here is student with a light case of bleeding gums. His dentist has instructed him to massage gums by placing little splinters of wood called Inter Dens between the teeth and massaging gum with seesaw motion. He snatches an Inter Dens, opens his mouth in a stiff grimace and jabs at a gum with a shaking hand. Now he remembers his DE. Start over. Take out the little splinters of wood like small chopsticks joined at the base and separate them gently. Now find where the bleeding is. Relax face and move Inter Dens up and down gently firmly gums relaxed direct your attention to that spot. No not "getting better and better" just let the attention of your whole body flow there and all the healing power of your body flow with it. A soapy hand on your lower back feeling the muscles and vertebrae can catch a dislocation right there and save you a visit to the osteopath. Illness and disability is largely a matter of neglect. You ignore something because it is painful and it becomes more uncomfortable through neglect and you neglect it further. Everyday tasks become painful and boring because you think of them as WORK something solid and heavy to be fumbled and stumbled over. Overcome this block and you will find that DE can be applied to anything you do even to the final discipline of doing nothing. The easier you do it the less you have to do.

He who has learned to do nothing with his whole mind and body will have everything done for him.

Let us now apply DE to a simple test: the old Western quick draw gun fight. Only one gun fighter really grasped the principle of DE and that one was Wyatt Earp. Nobody ever beat him. Wyatt Earp said: "It's not the first shot that counts. It's the first shot that hits. Point is to draw aim and fire and deliver the slug an inch above the belt buckle."

That's DE. How fast can you do it and get it done?

It is related that a young boy once incurred the wrath of Two Gun McGee. McGee has sworn to kill him and is even now preparing himself in a series of saloons. The boy has never been in a gun fight and Wyatt Earp advises him to leave town while McGee is still two saloons away. The boy refuses to leave.

"All right" Earp tells him "You can hit a circle four inches square at six feet can't you? All right *take your time and hit it*." Wyatt flattens himself against a wall calling out once more *"Take your time, kid."*

(How fast can you take your time, kid?)

At this moment McGee bursts through the door a .45 in each hand aspittin lead all over the town. A drummer from St Louis is a bit slow hitting the floor and catches a slug in the forehead. A boy peacefully eating chop suey in the Chinese restaurant next door stops a slug with his thigh.

Now the kid draws his gun steadies it in both hands aims and fires at six feet hitting Two Gun McGee squarely in the stomach. The heavy slug knocks him back against the wall. He manages to get off one last shot and bring down the chandelier. The boy fires again and sends a bullet ripping through McGee's liver and another through his chest.

The beginner can think of DE as a game. You are running an obstacle course the obstacles set up by your opponent. As soon as you attempt to put DE into practice you will find that you have an opponent very clever and persistent and resourceful with detailed knowledge of your weaknesses and above all expert in diverting your attention for the moment necessary to drop a plate on the kitchen floor. Who or what is this opponent that makes you spill drop and fumble slip and fall? Groddeck and Freud called it the IT a built in self-destructive mechanism. Mr Hubbard calls it the Reactive Mind. You will disconnect IT as you advance in the discipline of DE. DE brings you into direct conflict with the IT in present time where you can control your moves. You can beat the IT in present time.

Take the inverse skill of the IT back into your own hands. These skills belong to you. Make them yours. You *know* where the wastebasket is. You can land an object in that wastebasket over your shoulder. You *know* how to touch and move and pick up things. Regaining these physical skills is of course simply a prelude to regaining other skills and other knowledge that you have but cannot make available for your use. You *know* your entire past history just what year month day and hour everything happened. If you have heard a language for any length of time you *know* that language. You have a computer in your brain. DE will show you how to use it. But that's another chapter.

DE applies to ALL operations carried out inside

the body . . . brain waves, digestion, blood pressure
and rate of heart beats . . . And that's another chapter . . .

"And now I have stray cats to feed and my class
at the Leprosarium."

Lady Sutton-Smith raises a distant umbrella . . .

"I hope you find your way . . . The address in
empty streets . . ."

THE PERFECT SERVANT

John J Hudson, known as Basic J to his many friends, is making a difficult decision in the Pentagon. Word has just come through from B&C . . . complete, precise and permanent programming of thought feeling and sensory data demonstrated in experimental preparations after single exposure to Virus Rover this information conveyed in a three word inter office memo . . . rover is ready.

No further need to explain excuse produce any arguments or facts in support of departmental directives. It will soon be neurologically impossible to oppose or even to question. The virus is hereditary of course a permanent chromatic formula circuits of protest closed forever. Rover will see to that. Basic J has the responsibility of releasing rover in the United States of America. He looks up at Old Glory hanging over his desk. *American* programming of course . . . he will see to that. He gets up and paces around the room.

"Gotta stay ahead of the Commies . . . if they get there first with *their* programming . . . everybody's kids will speak Chinese at birth." This he decides grimly must be made unthinkable . . . "The President is right. The President is always right. The laws are right. America is right. America is always right. The American way of life is the right way of life is the best way of life is the only way of life" from here to eternity.

His duty is clear. He salutes Old Glory. His throat is dry. He rings for Bently the perfect servant a faithful old dog of that he is absolutely sure. The psyche department checked him out and he checked so clear they used some of his bone marrow in the rover cultures. Bently stands in the door.

"Yes sir?"

"A glass of ice water please Bently."

"Yes sir."

With the speed of a conjurer Bently places a glass of ice water on a brocade napkin. "Good old Bently always knows what I need."

The perfect servant he draws the curtains. "Anything else sir?"

"No nothing else. Good night Bently."

"Good night Mr Hudson. Good bye Mr Hudson."

"What was that Bently?" Hudson put down the half empty glass.

"Good bye Mr Hudson." For a moment Bently looks at him with something like emotion. He bows and leaves the room.

Hudson drains his glass. He sits for some time in silent thought.

Suddenly he knows what to do. Reverently he spreads Old Glory on the desk. He picks up a pen right to hand somehow and ready by a piece of parchment paper. He writes.

Dear Mary

I am taking the only way out. Please forgive me.

Basic J Hudson

Spring drawer cold .45 . . . "It's the right thing to do it's the best thing to do it's the only thing to do . . . good old Bently . . . he knew somehow . . ."

"I was on the way back to my room sir when I heard the shot sir. I found him like that sir." He nods to the desk. The side of Hudson's face is stuck to Old Glory in a paste of dry blood and seared brains. "I saw at once he was dead sir."

"You can say that again" said the agent.

"It was a terrible shock for me sir."

There are two agents in the room two very special agents. They both turn and look at Bently in a very special way.

"You expect us to swallow this crap?"

Bently draws himself up. "I have told you the truth sir exactly as it happened sir."

"And I say it's crap. Do we have to bake it out of you Bently?" Bently takes a deep breath. A button pops from his waistcoat and explodes against the agent's grey flannel suit.

"Will that be all sir?"

"Yes Bently. You may go."

"Thank you sir." Bently bows and leaves the room.

(Long pause)

"Well that puts him in the clear . . . Good old Bently."

"You can say that again. Old Bently has all the answers. Old Bently has all the right answers. If anybody says or even thinks different I'll gun the bastard down if he's my best buddy."

"I was on the way back to my room sir when I heard the shots sir. I found the two gentlemen like that sir." He nods to the floor. "I saw at once they were dead sir. Blood and internals all over the room sir. A smell of blood and excrement sir. If you'll pardon the expression sir. Quite overwhelming sir."

"You may go Bently."

"Thank you sir. I'll be in my room if you need me sir."

"Better check that guy out."

"You can say that again. Hey here's something." He picks up the pen with forceps and reads

For James Bently in recognition of ten years faith-ful service to John J Hudson

He removes the cap from the pen. There is a slight explosion followed by a long reverent silence.

"If J thought that much of him he must be all right," the agent bursts out in a voice hoarse with emotion. He turns away to hide the tears in his eyes. Another agent chokes and buries his face in a curtain wracked with sobs.

"Oh what the Hell" screams the CIA man "it's nothing to be ashamed of. Let's cry our decent American hearts out and for the Christ sake let's all get fried." He rushes the liquor cabinet and tosses bottles out to his colleagues.

"I was on the way back to my room sir when I heard the noise sir. Quite indescribable sir. I felt it my duty to return sir. I found them reeling about sir.

Screaming 'good old Bently' sir. That gentleman" he points to the CIA man who is slumped in a chair between two guards sobbing out "Auld Lang Syne" "threw himself on me in a most offensive way sir. If you'll pardon the expression sir and said nearly as I can recall sir would I be his 'crying cousin' sir. Old southern custom he said it was sir. I could see he'd been drinking sir."

"Bently doesn't it strike you a bit odd that thirty of the most trusted and responsible officials in this country should with one accord and for no discernible reason become maudlin drunk over a period of two minutes?"

"That is not for me to say sir."

"You have testified that the men were quite normal when you left the room."

"Yes sir. Whatever happened sir happened after I had left the room sir."

"Things always seem to happen after you leave rooms Bently."

"Not always sir."

The new department head looks at Bently and his jaw drops.

"Why the man is smiling or snarling rather in a strange animal way. What the Hell?"

"ACHOO ACHOO ACHOOOOOOOO"

"BLESS YOU BENTLY BLESS YOU BLESS YOU"

"ACHOO ACHOO ACHOOOOOOOO"

"BLESS YOU SIR BLESS YOU BLESS YOU"

"Let's all go ACHOO ACHOO out into the BLESS YOU BLESS YOU beautiful American ACHOO

ACHOO streets and BLESS YOU BLESS YOU bless all our fellow ACHOO ACHOO Americans BLESS YOU ACHOOOOOOOO"

Sneezing and blessing they rushed into the street. Alone in the room Bently wipes off the grey features of a perfect servant to reveal himself as the Insidious Doctor Fu Manchu. He steps to the window.

"ACHOO ACHOO" The cities and towns of America echo back

"BLESS YOU BLESS YOU"

"ACHOO ACHOO" back from the farms crossroads and lonely sidings of "BLESS YOU BLESS YOU"

"ACHOO ACHOO" on the winds of Panhandle idiot honky tonks yodel back "BLESS YOU BLESS YOU ALLAYIHOO"

From car and plane "ACHOO ACHOO" Hell's Angels roaring back "BLESS YOU BLESS YOU"

America America "ACHOO ACHOO ACHOO" from purple mountain's majesty "BLESS YOU BLESS YOU BLESS YOU"

The doctor stands at the window waiting.

"Achoo achoo" with wind and dust "bless you bless you"

"Achoo achoo" a hoarse whisper echoes back "bless you bless you"

"Achoo achoo" spitting blood "bless you bless you"

Old record running down "achoo achoo achoo"

Dying dying dying "bless you bless you bless you"

The doctor's silent blessing falls on silent cities from sea to shining sea.

ALI'S SMILE

The set is a country house, young man with briefcase at the door. The door is opened by a grey-haired man dressed in a blue dressing gown.

"Yes?"

"I am your local Scientologist . . . what can I do for you?"

"Drop Dead!"

The door slams. The man, Clinch Smith, totters back to the living room and collapses on the sofa.

The set is crater-like valley in the suburbs of a middle-sized English city. There are authentic cottages with moss on the roofs. There is "Ye Olde Bramble Tye Motel," high prices, thin walls.

Over the valley towers a vast grey slag heap, a mine tip. The camera moves at a purposeful trot. A peasant steps placidly in a field. Huntsmen in red coats have stepped from a print in "Ye Olde Marl Hole Tavern." An eccentric Lesbian attacks them with her umbrella. She is cheered on by hippies.

Now uncouth local youth erupt from "Ye Olde Marl Hole Tavern"; and soon fights are in progress between the hippies and the locals.

Smith reread the letter. "Your flippant attitude toward Scientology makes you a *down-stat, suppressive* person. I disconnect from you. Don't ever get on my comlines again. Harry."

Clinch buried his face in his hands, sobbing. "Ingrates, every one of them ingrates, why I *paid* for his Scientology courses." He looked up through his histrionic tears and there was Ali's kris on the wall.

It was thirty years ago in Malaya. The first time he saw Ali was in the market. He noticed a crowd, curiously divided, the men sullen and downcast, the women laughing and radiant. He pushed through the crowd and there in the center of the circle was a slender boy of eighteen dressed in a curtain, his face crudely made-up. In front of him a toothless old hag does a toothless obscene dance. He imitates her every movement.

Looking into the boy's eyes Clinch saw that he was helpless in there, watching in agony what his body was doing. He was, in fact, a *Latah,* that is a condition where the victim must imitate every movement, once his attention has been attracted by a special signal.

"My God" Clinch thought. "Suppose one has to let a fart in front of the Queen? His body doesn't belong to him. "Stop this!" he said firmly in the thundering tones of an English Lesbian preventing some rude tribesman from maltreating a donkey. The old hag shot him a look of such malevolence he felt the hair stir on the back of his neck. She spat out the Malay word for "queer" in Betel Nut.

Clinch made Ali his houseboy and gave him an amulet to protect him from the market woman.

That morning Clinch woke up with a malarial headache to find he was out of codeine. He sent Ali to the market and arranged to meet him at eleven in the British Chemist. The door of Ali's room was open and there on the table was the amulet. Clinch felt a sudden chill. "Probably malaria" he thought. He slipped the amulet into his pocket and set off for the chemist, his head pounding in the morning sun. He would ask for water and take two pills in the chemist's, he decided, looking forward to the cool shop, the water, the codeine.

Someone laid a hand on his arm. He turned around, annoyed, and looked into blue eyes that twinkled a warning. It was a bearded archeologist who had always been mysteriously friendly. He was about to plead an appointment and break away but the man looked at him steadily.

"You're interested in linguistics, thought you might like to have a look at this . . ."

There was no stopping the fellow and the clipping *was* interesting, he saw that at a glance. It was relative to a theory Clinch had written to the effect that every language had a particular cadence or rhythm that could be reduced to a neutral musical score. This score, once learned, would literally pull the language into the student's mind.

This thesis was coldly received by his superiors; and Clinch's obtuse persistence in pushing it finally resulted in a penal assignment in La Paz. An inheritance from an uncle saved him sitting out years of ignominity writing for his pension.

As he read the clipping he heard the clock strike

eleven in the market. He finished the clipping and handed it back. As he turned into the market he heard the cry "Amok! Amok! Amok!" And there was Ali with his kris in front of the drugstore. The shutters fell like a guillotine. The old market women were scampering off with the agility of rats or evil spirits. Three of them were too slow.

And now Ali was running straight toward him, face blazing like a comet. Clinch Smith stood up. He felt the hair stir on the back of his neck and a shiver spattered his body with goose pimples.

"Ali! Ali! Ali!"

He walked over and took the kris from the wall. It seemed to leap into his hand. He opened the door and started for the Scientology Center, moving with a purposeful trot, the kris held in front of him.

And then the shots. Three heavy slugs tore into Ali's body and he kept coming. Three more bullets cut him down and he fell at Clinch's feet. Sun helmet, shorts, the lean bronze face.

He shoved the Webley .455 automatic revolver into his holster and buttoned it in. It is, far as I know, the only automatic revolver ever made. There are ratchings in the cylinder so that each shot turns the cylinder and recocks the revolver. It was sold as the fastest handgun ever made.

("Come along to the club, old man. You could do with a drink." The officer turned. The policeman had approached reluctantly; and the officer gave him some orders in crisp Malay.)

Clinch Smith: "I'd like the kris as a souvenir, you understand. He was my houseboy."

"Oh, yes, of course, old chap. Quite understand. I'll have it sent along to your digs."

The Scientologist, meanwhile, whose name was Reg, walked away in a down-stat condition. He could feel his gains ebbing away in the afternoon streets that were suddenly full of raw menace that seemed to bounce off walls and windows. The arc was flowing out of him and he felt a terrible weakness. He feared the sin of self-invalidation.

"I must up-stat myself" he told himself, firmly. "I'll make a report to Ethics." He swayed and steadied himself on a tree. Silver spots boiled in front of his eyes. He turned a corner, and there, just ahead, a knot of people. Accident, fight perhaps, here was a chance to prove himself. Perhaps he could save a little girl from dying of burns with a brilliant touch-assist. The words of Ron came back to him: "In any kind of emergency, just *be there,* saying firmly 'You are standing in my space.' " And while the wogs think that over he is past them and right up to the front where he sees some hippies fighting with local youths and landed gentry. He looked up and caught his breath. Five members of the Sea Org resplendent in blue uniforms shoved their way through the crowd.

"Hey, you're not proper boogies." A gang of boys from Glasgow were closing in, slow hands caressing switchblades in their pockets.

Lord Westfield had been born intelligent, at the same time very rich. This unusual occurrence of retrograde planetary juxtapositions, all agree it was a radioactive day, when everything is ugly and menacing street boys scream insults. Mules foaled and the hooded deal did gibber in the streets in Clayton, Missouri. Four schoolboys caught jacking off by MacIntosh the druggist who is a self-styled sodomy fighter and goes around looking for the bastards, screaming "I will DRAAAG you to the police" got five years for sodomy. In Mississippi they strung a nigger up under a railroad bridge, burning his genitals off with a blowtorch.

The face of the man with the torch? "Well, we dressed him up in Esquire clothes, it became the *new* look, the *bold* look. And he was a pretty hot property. Now, we had an exclusive on this good thing; and I happened to remember the day was one thing like that after the other.

"A woman bit the cock off her husband because he was queer; and her copper-loving brother stomped him to death."

Now, had Lord Westfield been born under any other circumstances, he would undoubtedly have been successful. From an early age he observed the deference paid him by the townspeople. He was not stupid enough to think this was his by some mysterious right. Lord Westfield disliked mysteries. A mystery is an unknown factor and therefore dangerous. He could see these people were cowed and broken; but he wanted to know exactly how this had been done so he could make sure such a desirable state of affairs would continue.

As a child and adolescent he amused himself by seeing how many insults and humiliations he could inflict on the local villagers. "Always" he told himself "inflict as much damage as you possibly can on anyone you encounter. If you leave him feeling worse than when you saw him, something of value has been accomplished."

To this end he betook himself to secret studies and employed a firm of private investigators who were glad to do anything for his Lordship, who never forgot them on Christmas and no questions asked.

"Go look into this and that. See what Doctor Miller has to say. You have journalistic credentials . . . Scientists are very absent-minded, thank God. Get me the data on Scientology."

The agent dumps a pile of books and pamphlets on Lord Westfield's desk. Lord Westfield leafs through a book. Wearily he sweeps the pile of books to the floor.

"This isn't what I want . . . this illiterate drivel . . . I want the course material, I want *all* of it, on the market or in preparation. You understand me?"

"You mean I have to go and take courses sir? Why not just lift the lot?"

The firm of Jenkins and Coldbourne were experts in gaining access to premises, photographing and replacing documents. They had done a number of these jobs for Lord Westfield with exemplary efficiency.

"No, I want you to go and take the courses. Then I want you to come back here and run through it with me, day by day, you understand?"

"They'll smell me out on the E-meter, if you'll pardon the expression sir. They have this lie detector sir. You can't beat it sir. You see, I did a job for them once . . . my wife took a personal efficiency course at the London Center and that's how I got into it. Well, I padded my expense account a bit; and this grim old biddy drags me into a broom closet, puts me on the cans, and says should I have told her anything I didn't.

"That reads, what do you think *this* could mean. She bloody dragged it out of me sir, and said I would have to wear a grey rag sir, and go around and ask every decent Scientologist if I could rejoin the group. I quit sir."

"Don't worry about sec-checks, all you need to do is take one of these." Lord Westfield shoves a bottle of pills across the table. "Sit down, Jenkins, and stop pretending to be stupider than you are. Now this drug lowers the electrical resistance of the brain."

Now Jenkins has dropped his obsequious cockney voice. "Yes sir, of course. The E-meter works on resistance."

"I believe that electronics is a hobby of yours, Jenkins?"

"Yes sir, in fact I've been working on an E-meter that'll work on *non*-resistance."

"Have you really? When you get it finished, bring it along, perhaps the Technical Department will be interested. Now, on this assignment you have to watch every word and every move. There isn't a man or woman in the org won't turn you in if you so much as nip into a bar for half a pint on course, so for Christ's sake, don't get caught out taking a pill!"

"I used to give sleight-of-hand shows in the Council Hall sir. I was on the junk in New York. I know ten different ways of getting a pill into my mouth under closed-circuit TV"

Of course, Lord Westfield knew all this and a lot more about Jenkins. Intelligence during the war, electronics and demolitions expert, expert at gaining access to premises, photographing and returning documents, & expert in electronic spying devices.

"And remember this, Jenkins, you're going to have to study. It's a tough course, they tell me."

Jenkins went pale . . . "You don't mean I have to take the special briefing course sir?"

"No, Jenkins, just what you need to get the clearing course, then you can lift the rest."

Two weeks later when Jenkins showed up for the daily lesson, he looked worried . . . "Lord Westfield, it's them pills sir."

"Yes, Jenkins?"

"Well, if you'll pardon the expression sir, they loosen my rectum sir. I've had, er, several accidents sir. You see, there's been a scandal about the confidential material; and they've gone sec-check mad sir. It's a side-effect."

"Well, Jenkins, you can lift the rest."

Scientology was one of the many subjects that interested Lord Westfield. On the surface he was a highly placed but obscure civil servant at the Home Office. There were select dinners for highly placed officials . . . Lord Westfield, who was on his way to a Top Secret meeting with Olga Hardcastle, looked out the one-way window of his Bentley and saw that a fight was in progress. He stopped the car, got out and sat on his cane seat to watch the fight.

Two middle-aged women were the first to notice Clinch Smith. They looked at the kris in disapproval

. . . "He's not allowed to carry that." She didn't have time to scream. He ripped her stomach open, striking from near the ground. The other looked at him, her face flapping in silent terror. He swung his arm and cut her throat.

He turned to face the crowd. Electric menace blazing from his kris, which vibrated with a life of its own, pulling him down a funnel of screaming, running figures. And there, at the end of the funnel, is the Sea Org, Lord Westfield, and Olga.

The Sea Org has something eccentric and puritanical in their dress, like MRA personnel. They placed themselves in ineffectual karate stance.

When Lord Westfield saw Clinch Smith's face, he knew he was a dead man. He had studied karate, Chinese boxing, judo, aikido. He was giving the orders to his hand, but a numbing paralysis clutched him. Suddenly he broke through, his limbs stiff with panic, brought the cane seat up in a clumsy stab to the groin.

Clinch seemed to undulate aside, as if the ground had moved under his feet, straightened his bent arm, rippling the kris along the side of Lord Westfield's throat. He straightened his arm and shoved the kris right into Olga's open mouth and out the back of her neck. He placed his left hand on her face and shoved, snapping the kris in an arc that nearly decapitated a Sea Org member.

Whirling, dancing, shifting . . . he slashed and stabbed.

Crack.

Colonel Wentworth stood there with a sporting rifle.

Born Marvin Weinstein he sported a dubious military title from World War II. His first shot killed Lord Westfield's chauffeur. He moved closer.

Crack.

Clinch Smith fell under a pile of dead Sea Org uniforms. Meanwhile, a rumor has flashed through the town that the Home Secretary has ordered a massacre of hippies and militants. Now they come out in droves, all marching toward the scene of battle just ahead. This is it.

They glimpse a slender young Malay boy, a Negro, a Mexican, a Chinese, perhaps, crushed under a pile of cops. Pulling baseball bats and bicycle chains, they charge. Many of the opposition fainted at the sight; and the weaker ones had heart attacks.

What remained summoned something so ugly that several hippies with Zen leanings faltered and said "Let's talk this over." But the stronger hippies were strengthened and their eyes blazed while the embattled police and landed gentry flung themselves forward.

"You filthy bastards are asking for it!"

And now the two hosts are approaching each other. Then a sound like falling mountains . . .

"The Tip! The Tip! The Tip!"

A wall of grey mud, twenty feet tall, is sweeping into the valley.

Next shot shows a lunar landscape of fluid slag.

Against the icy blackness of space, the ghost face of Ali . . . smiles.

TWILIGHT'S LAST GLEAMINGS

This film concerns a conspiracy to blow up a train carrying nerve gas from the west coast to the east coast where it is supposed to be dumped into the Atlantic. *The conspiracy is not political.* Only one FBI man is alert to the danger and he cannot convince his superiors that a conspiracy exists. He is playing a hunch and sometimes he doubts the validity of his intuition. Minutes before countdown he has the evidence he needs. He gets through to the President. Army, Navy, Marines converging on headquarters of the conspirators. FBI man rounds up local police and leads raiding party. Raiding party and conspirators wiped out. Marines, Army, Navy rush in through a pile of corpses and deactivate the robot-controlled missile that is designed to blow up the train. Conspiracy succeeds posthumously when a truck driver on LSD trip with a load of high octane gas crashes into the train.

Conspirators include a folksy meteorologist, an embittered homosexual, a Chinese camera man, a Lesbian, a Mexican *pistolero,* a Negro castrated in his cradle by rat bites. The time and place for countdown depends of course on prevailing winds and the meteorologist is busy with continual calculations, weather maps, barometer and wind reads, telescopic observation of clouds and birds. There are also instruments of his own invention. He is contemptuous of weather reports. "Doesn't know a typhoon from a fart. You see that vulture up yonder? He can tell you more than a room full of weather maps and barometers. The birds know."

As the conspirators move across the country the FBI man is always one step behind them. His investigations are handicapped by his belief that the conspiracy is political which sends him down a number of false trails.

Actually the conspiracy is financed by a private inheritance. This sum was left to Clem the meteorologist by an eccentric billionaire perturbed by overpopulation, air and water pollution, and the destruction of wild life.

BILLIONAIRE (on his deathbed): "Clem, swear to me by everything we both hold sacred that you will use every cent of that money to turn the clock back to 1899 when a silver dollar bought a good meal or a good piece of ass."

Opening scene shows Old Glory in the wind seen through Telstar. "Star-Spangled Banner" is playing. Cut to conspirators headquarters in run-down 1920 bungalow. There are weather maps on the wall and a relief map of the U.S.A.

CLEM (looking up from Telstar): "Now I just wish that breeze would hold up for another 48 hours."

Audrey the homosexual is looking through the Telstar . . . U.S. Army Reservation. Authorized Persons Only. Inside the gate the last cylinders of nerve gas are being loaded into a train. The Telstar lingers lovingly on the ass of a young soldier who is bending over to pick up a cylinder of gas.

Cut back to headquarters. Mr. Lee the Chinese camera man takes over at the Telstar. Train doors shut and locked. A gum-chewing MP reading *Sextoons* presses a button. The gates open and the train moves out.

CLEM (standing in front of U.S.A. map): "You know I love this country. Only thing wrong with it is the folks living there." (His face goes black with hate.) "MOTHER-LOVING STUPID-ASSED BIBLE-BELT CUNTSUCKERS." (He smiles and turns to Audrey, Miss Longridge and the spade whose name is Jones.) "Now you're city folk. You never drank cool spring water on a summer afternoon. You never sat down to fried squirrel and jack salmon with black-eyed peas and wild raspberries. You never planted corn and cotton and tomatoes and watched them grow. You never sank your hands in the soil and let it run through your fingers . . . sandy loam . . . I've seen it four feet deep . . ." (He turns back to the map.) "Yes sir we're gonna lay down a mighty fine load of fertilizer." (He sweeps his hand across the Middle West.) "The trees will grow again, the bison will come back, the deer and the wild turkey."

JONES: "I had a dream he said."

AUDREY: "Other people are different from me and I don't like them."

The camera man is taking shots through the Telstar. Miss Longridge is looking at the nudes in *Playboy*. Tío Mate the Mexican *pistolero* is cleaning his Smith & Wesson tip-up .44. It is a beautiful custom-made gun with hunting scenes engraved on the cylinder and barrel given to him by the *patrón* thirty years ago for "taking care of my unfortunate brother the General." Jones is taking a fix.

Cut to FBI man pacing up and down in his office. His name is Joe Rogers.

ROGERS: "I had a dream I tell you. I saw that train go up and that gas sweeping up the Eastern seaboard."

His second in command Mr Falk is inclined to be cynical and describes himself as "a white-collar bum who works for that crazy American government."

FALK: "Are you going to tell the Chief about your dream, Joe?:"
ROGERS (picking up phone): "No but I'm going to ask him for more agents."
FALK: "Gotta stay ahead of the Commies or everybody's kids will be learning Chinese."
ROGERS: "If my hunch is correct there may not be any kids left to learn anything."

Cover story of the conspirators is that they are making a documentary film of America. Clem is the director, Lee the camera man, Audrey the script writer,

Miss Longridge the business manager and Tío Mate the studio guard. The film of course *is* a documentary of America. Theme songs: "The Star-Spangled Banner," "America I Love You," "From Sea to Shining Sea," "Don't Fence Me In," "Home on the Range," "The Red River Valley."

Rogers encounters the film company at the O.K. Corral in Tombstone. He is intuitively suspicious. However a check turns up no political connections and he drops the lead.

As the conspirators move from one set to the other following the train incidents occur.

In a deserted roadhouse Audrey rapes a young sailor at gunpoint while Lee impassively films the action.

AUDREY: "O.K. CUT . . ." (He turns to the sailor.) "You can put on your clothes now . . . And now let's see how fast you can run."

Sailor takes off like a rabbit and reaches the top of a hill fifty yards away. Tío Mate draws aims and fires. Tío Mate can blast a vulture out of the air with his .44.

Miss Longridge rapes two female hitchhikers. And then, stark naked, she kills them with a baseball bat.

They stop at a filling station and honk. Nobody comes so Jones gets out to fill the tank himself. At this moment the owner of the filling station, a Nigger-killing lawman with six notches in his gun, comes out a side door.

LAWMAN: "Get away from that pump, boy."
JONES: "Yahsuh boss." (He drenches the lawman with gasoline and sets him on fire.)

Jones who is hooked on junk leaves a wake of dead druggists.

Audrey is restrained at gun point from mass rape of a Boy Scout troop.

Tío Mate shoots down an army helicopter.

Clem sounds a word of warning to his impetuous companions.

CLEM: "Such a thing as too much fun. We're leaving a trail like a herd of elephants."

They are stopped by three cops who won't swallow the film play despite Clem's expert patter.

COP: "We gotta find out who you folks are."

Clem drops his hands resignedly and nods to Tío Mate.

TÍO MATE: "I will show you who we are *señores*." (He kills them with three shots.)

CLEM (getting out of the car): "Now how is this gonna look? Three cops right dead center between the eyes. I grant you it's funny haha but it's also damned funny peculiar."

They put the cops in their car set the car on fire and send it over a cliff.

A pattern is emerging . . . dead druggists. Helicopter pilot killed by .44 bullet . . . On a hunch Rogers runs autopsy on the three cops found in burned-out car. All three died from a heavy caliber bullet through the head . . . naked bodies of two female hitchhikers found under a railroad bridge their heads battered to jelly . . . young sailor killed by a .44 caliber bullet in the back . . . better dig him up too . . . recent sexual assault . . . Meanwhile reports are coming in . . . Government warehouse raided . . . large stock of atropine syrettes taken . . . Negroes, Puerto Ricans, Chinese, queers and Lesbians leaving the east coast in droves. Suddenly it hits him like lightning . . . THE DOCUMENTARY FILM COMPANY.

The day is September 17. Hurricane warning out. The film company is in an old deserted estate reconstructing the 1920s. Set is Palm Beach. Minutes to countdown . . . Outside the wind is rising.

Clem steps onto balcony and looks at the breakers smashing against the sea wall.

CLEM: "ZOWIE."

Rogers rushes into police headquarters in West Palm Beach.

ROGERS: "FBI. GET ME TO A PHONE."

He commandeers the entire police force of Palm Beach and West Palm Beach. Sirens blaring they race through the wind-torn streets. Trees are going now. A car full of cops is electrocuted by a high-tension wire. They sweep up the weed-grown driveway and surround the house. The conspirators are outnumbered ten to one but they have bazookas, grenade launchers, machine guns and phosgene bombs. As the battle rages the hurricane hits full force. When the Marines, the Army and the Navy arrive everybody is dead on both sides. Clem's hand is inches from the control switch.

FIVE STAR GENERAL: "Thank God we arrived in time." (He looks at the dead cops.) "And thank God for men like these." (He orders the bugler to play taps.)

Cut to the tripping truck driver coming down a long grade throttle to the floor the hurricane behind him. He bellows out "The Battle Hymn of the Republic."

HE HATH LOOSED THE FATAL LIGHTNING
OF HIS TERRIBLE SWIFT SWORD
HE IS TRAMPLING OUT THE VINTAGE WHERE
THE GRAPES OF WRATH ARE STORED
HE HAS SOUNDED FORTH THE TRUMPET
THAT SHALL NEVER CALL RETREAT

He smashes into the train. White hot gas cylinders explode high in the air. The hurricane races north whipping clouds of nerve gas across a torn silver sky.

Film closes with "The Star-Spangled Banner" played softly in a minor key as the camera shows aerial view of dead cities with flash close-ups through Telstar. The camera is farther and farther away the music always fainter. Last shot shows ghost faces of the conspirators against a gleaming empty sky. They wave and smile.

THE COMING OF THE PURPLE BETTER ONE

Saturday August 24, 1968: Arrive O'Hare Airport, Chicago. First visit in 26 years. Last in Chicago during the war where I exercised the trade of exterminator.

"Exterminator. Got any bugs lady?"

"The tools of your trade" said the customs officer touching my cassette recorder.

Driving in from the airport note empty streets newspapers in the wind a ghost town. Taxi strike bus strike doesn't account for the feeling of nobody here. Arrive Sheraton Hotel where I meet Jean Genet. He is dressed in an old pair of corduroy pants no jacket no tie. He conveys a remarkable impact of directness confronting completely whoever he talks to.

Sunday August 25: Out to the airport for the arrival of McCarthy. An estimated fifteen thousand supporters there to welcome him mostly young people. Surprisingly few police. Whole scene touching and ineffectual particularly in retrospect of subsequent events.

Monday August 26: We spend Monday morning in Lincoln Park talking to the Yippies. Jean Genet expresses himself succinctly on the subject of America and Chicago.

"I can't wait for this city to rot. I can't wait to see weeds growing through empty streets."

May not have to wait long. Police in blue helmets many of them wearing one-way dark glasses stand around heavy and sullen. One of them sidles up to me while I am recording and says: "You're wasting film."

Of course the sound track does bring the image track on set so there is not all that much difference between a recorder and a camera.

Another sidles up right in my ear. "They're talking about brutality. They haven't seen anything yet."

The cops know they are the heavies in this show and they are going to play it to the Hilton.

Monday night to the Convention Hall. Cobblestone streets smell of coal gas and stockyards. No place to park. Some citizen rushes out screaming. "You can't park here! I'll call the police! I'll have your car towed away!"

Through line after line of police showing our credentials and finally click ourselves in. Tinny atmosphere of carnivals and penny arcades without the attractions. The barkers are there but no freaks no sideshows no scenic railways.

Up to Lincoln Park where the cops are impartially clubbing Yippies newsmen and bystanders. After all there are no innocent bystanders. What are they doing here in the first place? The worst sin of man is to be born.

Tuesday August 27: The Yippies are stealing the show. I've had about enough of the convention farce without humor barbed wire and cops around a lot of nothing.

Jean Genet says: "It is time for writers to support the rebellion of youth not only with their words but with their presence as well."

It is time for every writer to stand by his words.

Lincoln Park Tuesday night: The Yippies have assembled at the epicenter of Lincoln Park. Bonfires, a cross, the demonstrators singing "The Battle Hymn of the Republic."

He hath loosed the fatal lightning of his terrible swift sword.

"Wet a handkerchief and put it in front of your face . . . Don't rub your eyes."

He is trampling out the vintage where the grapes of wrath are stored.

"Keep your cool and stay seated."

He has sounded forth the trumpet that shall never call retreat.

"Sit or split."

At this point I look up to see what looks like a battalion of World War I tanks converging on the youthful demonstrators and I say "What's with you Martin you wig already?"

He just looks at me and says: "Fill your hand stranger." And hauls out an old rusty police force from 1910 and I take off across Lincoln Park tear-gas canisters raining all around me. From a safe distance I turn around to observe the scene and see it as a 1917 gas attack from the archives. I make the lobby of the Lincoln Hotel where the medics are treating gas victims. The *Life-Time* photographer is laid out on a bench medics washing his eyes out. Soon he recovers and begins taking pictures of everything in sight. Outside the cops prowl about like aroused tomcats.

Wednesday August 28: Rally in Grant Park to organize a march to the Amphitheatre. I am impressed by the organization that has been built here. Many of the marshals wear crash helmets and blue uniforms. It is difficult to distinguish them from the police. Clearly the emergent Yippie uniform is crash helmet, shoulder pads, and aluminum jockstrap. I find myself in the second row of the nonviolent march feeling rather out of place since nonviolence is not exactly my program. We shuffle slowly forward the marshals giving orders over the loudspeaker.

"Link arms . . . Keep five feet between rows . . . You back there watch what you're smoking . . . Keep your cool . . . This is a nonviolent march . . . You can obtain tear-gas rags from the medics . . ."

We come to a solid line of cops and there is a confab between the cops and the marshals. For one horrible moment I think they will let us march five bloody miles and me with blisters already from walking around in the taxi strike. No. They won't let us march. And being a nonviolent march and five beefy cops for every marcher and not being equipped with bulldozers it is an impasse. I walk around the park recording and playing back, a beauteous evening calm and clear vapor trails over the lake youths washing tear gas out of their eyes in the fountain. Spot of bother at the bridge where the pigs and national guardians have stationed themselves like Horatio but in far greater numbers.

So out to the Convention Hall where they don't like

the look of us despite our electronic credentials being in order and call a Secret Service man for clearance. We get in finally and I play back the Grant Park recordings and boo Humphrey to while away the time as they count votes to the all too stupid and obvious conclusion.

What happened Wednesday night when the guard dogs broke loose again is history.

I have described the Chicago police as left over from 1910 and in a sense this is true. Daley and his nightstick authority date back to turn-of-the-century ward politics. They are anachronisms and they know it. This I think accounts for the shocking ferocity of their behavior. Jean Genet, who has considerable police experience, says he never saw such expressions before on allegedly human faces. And what is the phantom fuzz screaming from Chicago to Berlin, from Mexico City to Paris? "We are REAL REAL REAL!! REAL as this NIGHTSTICK!" As they feel, in their dim animal way, that reality is slipping away from them. Where are all the old cop sets Clancy? Eating your apple twirling your club the sky goes out against your back. Where are the men you sent up who came around to thank you when they got out? Where is the gold watch the chief gave you when you cracked the Norton case? And where are your pigeons Clancy? You used to be quite a pigeon fancier remember the feeling you got sucking arrests from your pigeons soft and evil like the face of your whiskey priest brother? Time to turn in your cop suit to the little Jew who will check it off in his book. Won't be needing you after Friday.

The youth rebellion is a worldwide phenomenon

that has not been seen before in history. I don't believe they will calm down and be ad execs at thirty as the establishment would like to believe. Millions of young people all over the world are fed up with shallow unworthy authority running on a platform of bullshit. There are five questions that any platform in America must answer not with hot air but with change on a basic level.

1. Vietnam: As I recollect the French were in there quite some years and finally pulled out to repeat the same mistake in Algeria. History tells us this is a war that cannot be won. Perhaps it is not intended to be won but merely as provocation and pretext to start a war with Red China. Looks like some folks figure the only answer to this mess is blow the set up and start over. May have happened several times before what we call history going back about 10,000 years and the human actor being about 500,000 years on set, give a little take a little, so what was he doing for the 480,000 years unaccounted for? If we have come from stone axes to nuclear weapons in ten thousand years this may well have happened before. Brion Gysin has put forward the theory that a nuclear disaster in what is now the Gobi desert destroyed the civilization that had made such a disaster possible and incidentally gave rise to what he terms "Albino freaks," namely the white race. Any case if we don't want to see the set go America should get out of Vietnam and reach an immediate agreement with Red China.

2. Alienated youth: The only establishment that is supported by its young people is Red China. And that is why the State Department does not want Americans to go there. They do not want Americans to realize that any establishment offering young people anything at all will get their support. Because the western establishments are not offering anything. They have nothing to declare but their bad intentions. Let them come all the way out in the open with their bad intentions, declare a Secret Service overwhelming majority, and elect a purple-assed baboon to the Presidency. At this dark hour in the history of the penny arcade, Wednesday troubling all our hearts, the aggressive Southern ape suh fought for you in the perilous Kon-Tiki Room of the Sheraton.

3. Black Power: Find out what they want and give it to them. All the signs that mean anything indicate that the blacks were the original inhabitants of this planet. So who has a better right to it?

4. Our police and judicial system: What would happen if all the cotton-picking, stupid-assed, bible-belt laws passed by bourbon-soaked state legislators were actually enforced together with all federal and city laws? If every businessman who chiseled on his income tax by one dollar was caught and jailed? If every drug offender was caught and jailed? If every violator of all the laws penalizing sex acts between consenting adults in private was caught and jailed? How many people would be in jail? I think 30,000,000 is a very conservative estimate. And how many cops would it take to detect and arrest these criminals? And how many guards to keep them confined? And how many judges parole officers and court personnel to process them? And how much money would this cost?

Fix yourself on 30,000,000 violators in vast internee camps all united to scream with the inflexible authority of one big mouth. "We want gymnasiums! Libraries! Swimming pools! We want golf courses! Country clubs! Theaters!"

And with every concession they scream for MORE! MORE! MORE!

"The internee delegation in a meeting with the President today demanded as a prerequisite for any talks the 'immediate and unconditional removal of the so-called guards.' "

Senator Bradly rose in the Senate to question the wisdom of setting up what he termed "a separate state of dubious loyalty at the very core of our nation."

"We want tanks! Planes! Submarines!"

"An ominous atmosphere smogged the capital today as peace talks with the internee delegation bogged down."

"We want a space program! We want an atom bomb!"

"The number of internees is swelling ominously . . . forty million . . . fifty million . . . sixty million . . . 'America is a thin shell around a pulsing core of sullen violators.' "

"Today the internees exploded their first atom bomb described as 'a low yield nuclear device.' "

"It may be low yield but it's right on our back porch" said Senator Bradly plaintively.

"Today the internees signed a mutual assistance pact with Red China."

As regards our judicial system there are three alternatives:

A. Total enforcement. Is either of our distinguished candidates for the Presidency prepared to support the computerized police terror that such enforcement would entail?

B. An admission that the judicial system is a farce and the laws not really intended to be enforced except in a haphazard sporadic fashion. Is either candidate prepared to make such an admission?

C. Get some bulldozers in here and clean out all this garbage and let no state saloon reel to his drunken feet and start braying about State rights. Is either candidate prepared to advocate the only sensible alternative?

5. *The disappearing dollar:* 1959 Minutes To Go: "I'm absolutely weak I can only just totter home the dollar has collapsed." Figuring ten years time lag the dollar should collapse in 1969. There is something wrong with the whole concept of money. It takes always more and more to buy less and less. Money is like junk. A dose that fixes on Monday won't fix on Friday. We are being swept with vertiginous speed into a worldwide inflation comparable to what happened in Germany after World War I. The rich are desperately stockpiling gold, diamonds, antiques, paintings, medicines, food, liquor, tools and weapons. Any platform that does not propose the basic changes necessary to correct these glaring failures is a farce. What is happening in America today is something that has never happened before in recorded history: *Total confrontation.* The lies are obvious. The machinery is laid bare. All Americans are being shoved by the deadweight of a broken control machine right in front of each other's faces. Like

it or not they cannot choose but see and hear each other.
How many Americans will survive a total confront?

In Last Resort the Truth

The scene is Grant Park Chicago 1968. A full-scale
model of *The Mayflower* with American flags for sails
has been set up. A.J. in his Uncle Sam suit steps to a
mike on the deck.

"Ladies and gentlemen it is my coveted privilege
and deep honor to introduce to you the distinguished
Senator and former Justice of the Supreme Court
Homer Mandrill known to his many friends as the
Purple Better One. No doubt most of you are familiar
with a book called *African Genesis* written by Robert
Ardrey a native son of Chicago and I may add a
true son of America. I quote from Mr. Ardrey's pene-
trating work: 'When I was a boy in Chicago I attended
the Sunday School of a neighborhood Presbyterian
church. I recall our Wednesday-night meetings with the
simplest nostalgia. We would meet in the basement.
There would be a short prayer and a shorter benedic-
tion. And we would turn out all the lights and in total
darkness hit each other with chairs.'

"Mr Ardrey's early training tempered his character
to face and make known the truth about the origins
and nature of mankind. 'Not in innocence and not in
Asia was mankind born. The home of our fathers was
the African highland on a sky-swept savannah glowing with menace. The most significant of all our gifts
was the legacy bequeathed us by our immediate fore-
bears a race of terrestrial, flesh-eating, killer apes . . .
Raymond A. Dart of the University of Johannesburg

was the strident voice from South Africa that would prove the southern ape to be the human ancestor. Dart put forward the simple thesis that Man emerged from the anthropoid background for one reason only: because he was a killer. A rock, a stick, a heavy bone was to our ancestral killer ape the margin of survival . . . And he said that since we had tried everything else we might in last resort try the truth . . . Man's original nature imposes itself on any human solution.'

"The aggressive southern ape suh, glowing with menace, fought your battles on the perilous veldts of Africa 500,000 years ago. Had he not done so you would not be living here in this great city in this great land of America raising your happy families in peace and prosperity. Who more fitted to represent our glorious Simian heritage than Homer Mandrill himself a descendant of that illustrious line? Who else can restore to this nation the spirit of true conservatism that imposes itself on any human solution? What candidate is better fitted for the highest office in the land at a time when this great republic is threatened by enemies foreign and domestic? Actually there can be only one candidate: the Purple Better One your future President."

To "The Battle Hymn of the Republic" an American flag is drawn aside revealing a purple-assed mandrill (thunderous applause). Led to the mike by Secret Service men in dark suits that bulge suggestively here and there the Purple Better One blinks in bewilderment.

The Technician mixes a bicarbonate of soda and belches into his hand. He is sitting in front of three instrument panels, one labeled P.A. for Purple Ass, one labeled A. for Audience, a third P. for Police. (Crude experiments with rhesus monkeys have demonstrated that small currents of electricity passed through electrodes into the appropriate brain areas can elicit any emotional or visceral response: rage, fear, sexuality, vomiting, sleep, defecation. No doubt with further experimentation these techniques will be perfected and electromagnetic fields will supersede the use of actual electrodes imbedded in the brain.) He adjusts dials as Homer's mouth moves to a dubbed speech from directional mikes. The features of other candidates are projected onto Homer's face from a laser installation across the park so that he seems to embody and absorb them all.

"At this dark hour in the history of the republic there are grave questions troubling all our hearts. I pledge myself to answer these questions. One question is the war in Vietnam which is not only a war but a holy crusade against the godless forces of international Communism. And I say to you if these forces are not contained they will engulf us all." (Thunderous applause.) "And I flatly accuse the administration of criminal diffidence in the use of atomic weapons. Are we going to turn a red white and blue ass to the enemy?" (No! No! No!) "Are we going to fight through to victory at any cost?" (Yes! Yes! Yes!) "I say to you we will win if it takes ten years. We will win if we have to police every blade of grass and every gook in Vietnam." (Thunderous applause.) "And after that we are going to wade in and take care of Chairman Mao and his gang of cutthroat slave drivers." (Thunderous applause.) "And if any country shall open its mouth to carp at the great American task well a single back-handed blow from our mighty Seventh Fleet will silence that impotent puppet of Moscow and Peking.

"Another question is so-called Black Power. I want to go on record as saying I am a true friend to all good Darkies everywhere." (To wild applause a picture of the world-famous statue in Natchitoches Louisiana flashes on screen. As you all know this statue shows a good old Darkie with his hat in his hand and is dedicated to All Good Darkies Everywhere.) Homer's voice chokes with emotion and tears drip off his purple nose. "Why when I was fourteen years old our old yard Nigrah Rover Jones got runned over by a laundry truck and I cried my decent American heart out. And I have a deep conviction that the overwhelming majority of Nigrahs in this country is good Darkies like Rover Jones. However we know that there is in this country today another kind of Nigrah and as long as there is a gas pump handy we all know the answer to that." (Thunderous applause.) "And I would like to say this to followers of the Jewish religion. Always remember we like nice Jews with Jew jokes. As for Nigger-loving Communistic agitating Sheenies well just watch yourself Jew boy or we'll cut the rest of it off." (That's telling em Homer.) What about the legalization of marijuana? "Marijuana! Marijuana! Why that's deadlier than cocaine. And what are we going to do about the vile America-hating hoodlums who call themselves hippies, Yippies, and chippies? We are going to put this scum behind bars like the animals they are." (Thunderous applause.) "And I'll tell you something else. A bunch of queers, dope freaks, and degenerated dirty writers is living in foreign lands under the protection of American passports from the vantage point of which they do not hesitate to spit their filth on Old Glory. Well we're going to pull the passports off those dope freaks." (The Technician pushes a sex button and the Simian begins to masturbate.) "Bring them back here and teach them to act like decent Americans." (The Simian emisses, hitting the lens of a *Life-Time* photographer.) "And I denounce as Communist-inspired the rumors that the dollar collapsed in 1959. I pledge myself to turn the clock back to 1899 when a silver dollar bought a steak dinner and good piece of ass." (Thunderous applause as a plane writes September 17, 1899, across the sky in smoke.) "I have heard it said that this is a lawless nation that if all the laws in this land were truly enforced we would have thirty percent of the population in jail and the remaining seventy percent on the cops. I say to you if there is infection in this great land it must be cut out by the roots. We will not fall into slack-assed permissive anarchism. I pledge myself to uphold the laws of America and to enforce these hallowed statutes on all violators regardless of race, color, creed or position." (Thunderous applause.) "We will overcome all our enemies foreign and domestic and stay armed to the teeth for years, decades, centuries."

A phalanx of blue-helmeted cops shoulder through the crowd. They stop in front of the deck. The lead cop looks up at A.J. and demands: "Let's see your permits for that purple-assed son of a bitch."

"Permits? We don't have any permits. We don't have to show you any stinking permits. You are talking suh to the future President of America."

The lead cop takes a slip of paper from his shirt pocket and reads *Municipal Code of Chicago* . . . Chapter 98, Section 14: "No person shall permit any dangerous animal to run at large, nor lead any such animal with a chain, rope, or other appliance, whether such animal be muzzled or unmuzzled, in any public way or public place." He folds the paper and shoves it back into his shirt pocket. He points at the Purple Better One. "It's dangerous and we got orders to remove it."

A cop steps forward with a net. The Technician shoves the rage dial all the way up. Screaming, farting, snarling, the Simian leaps off the deck onto the startled officer who staggers back and goes down thrashing wildly on the ground while his fellow pigs stand helpless and baffled not daring to risk a shot for fear of killing their comrade. Finally the cop heaves himself to his feet and throws off the Simian. Panting, bleeding, he stands there his eyes wild. With a scream of rage the Purple Better One throws himself at another patrolman who fires two panicky shots which miss the Simian and crash through a window of the Hilton in the campaign headquarters of a conservative Southern candidate. A photographer from the London *Times* is riddled with bullets by Secret Service men under the misconception he has fired from a gun concealed in his camera. The cop throws his left arm in front of his face. The Simian sinks his canines into the cop's arm. The cop presses his gun against the

Simian's chest and pumps in four bullets. Homer Mandrill thuds to the bloody grass, ejaculates, excretes and dies. A.J. points a finger at the cop.

"Arrest that pig!" he screams. "Seize the assassin!"

A.J. was held in $100,000 bail which he posted in cash out of his pocket. Further disturbances erupted at the funeral when a band of vigilantes who call themselves the White Hunters attempted to desecrate the flag-draped body as it was carried in solemn procession through Lincoln Park on the way to its final resting place in Grant Park. The hoodlums were beaten off by A.J.'s elite guard of Korean karate experts. The Daughters of the American Revolution who had gathered in front of the Sheraton to protest the legalization of marijuana were charged by police screaming "Chippies! Chippies! Chippies!" And savagely clubbed to the sidewalk in a litter of diamonds, teeth, blood, mink stoles and handbags.

As the Simian was laid to rest under a silver replica of *The Mayflower* a statue of the Purple Better One in solid gold at the helm, A.J. called for five minutes of silent prayer in memory of our beloved candidate, "Cut down in Grant Park by the bullets of an assassin . . . A Communistic Jew Nigger inflamed to madness by injections of marijuana . . . The fact that the assassin had, with diabolical cunning, disguised himself as a police officer indicates the workings of a far-flung Communistic plot the tentacles of which may reach into the White House itself. This foul crime shrieks to high heaven. We will not rest until the higher-ups are brought to justice whoever and wherever they may be. I pledge myself to name a suitable and worthy successor. We will overcome. We will realize the aspirations and dreams that every American cherishes in his heart. The American dream can be must be and will be realized. I say to you that Grant Park will be a shrine for all future Americans. In the words of the all-American poet James Whitcomb Riley

'Freedom shall a while repair
'To dwell a weeping hermit there.' "

"WHAT WASHINGTON? WHAT ORDERS?"

Old Sarge: "All right you Limey has-been I'm going to say it country simple. You have been taken over like a Banana Republic. Your royal family is nothing but a holograph picture projected by the CIA. What is its purpose? Well what is the purpose of the Pope for you Catholics good and bad standing with John 23 like a good soldier in the presence of your captain. Any way you slice it it's a grovel operation the way we like to see them I mean what we are doing while the Pope and the other Holies keep the marks paralyzed with grovel rays is one of mysteries you cannot understand the mercy of God we don't intend to be here when this shithouse goes up maybe I'm talking too much about private things family matters you might say and that's what we call the good old CIA the Family. When the prodigal son creeps back disillusioned from Peking.

Information known.

Expel barbarian.

Well the Family will forgive him if he is sincere in his hear on a lie detector . . .

"Well we're going to take you back."

The old ham fixes him with blue eyes like steel in sunlight

"Just don't ever let us down again."

From here to eternity the old game of war. Where would the Family be without it? So we can whittle off a little something to keep the royal family projected in Limey Land can't we now? So the Queen needs more money? Well humm call a story conference . . . Just how are we slanting this B.J.?"

B.J. (Doodling muscle boys) . . . "Nothing new. Just keep it going. They do need more money otherwise they will go down in the same spiral as everybody else and they wouldn't be the royal family any more could wind up in a semidetached in Darlington. They are supposed to be a supernatural family religious figures in fact and the more potent in that they are not acknowledged as such. Just ask an upper-class English about the royal family and he goes all huffy and vague

"It's not important . . ."

"Who *cares* about Philip."

"Can't stand that chap Tony."

"But you want the royal family to continue as such?"

(B.J. bulges a jockstrap)

"Well uh yes we are a *monarchy* . . . excuse me . . ."

"What about this million a year?"

"We're all together in this . . . couldn't abolish titles and keep the royal family . . . We've had to take cuts . . . Why shouldn't they take a cut too . . ."

Mutiny in the ranks? . . . (He doodles a boy pealing off plastic tits) It could come to that . . . (He doodles a boy looking at another boy's ass. A light bulb attached to his head lights up) . . . So why not put the royal family in a Darlington semidetached on a middle-class income and let them prove themselves in a TV serial . . .

Philip and the Queen are doing all right. She is known as Queen to all the nabors where she runs a small grocery shop. Every customer receives the same gracious smile and quick inquiry as to the family she is good at remembering things like that and keeping a line moving at the same time she learned that shaking millions of hands. Philip sells ecology equipment to factories . . . Good at his work and believes in it . . . strong middle-class message there Charles is a successful pop singer. Why they all get knighted in the end one way or another and the wind-up is back in Buckingham stronger than ever . . .

CIA Black: "Don't you think there is some limit somewhere to what people will stand still for? Suppose the ecology equipment doesn't work? Suppose the Queen's gracious smile is reserved for her white customers she has eyes for Enoch Powell and flying saucers . . . Suppose Bonny Prince Charlie . . ."

"For Chrisakes we're building them up not down . . . the *Family* . . ."

"All right call in the special effects boys and give them supernatural powers . . ."

"Never go too far in any direction is the basic rule on which Limey Land is built. The Queen stabilizes the whole sinking shithouse . . ."

"I tell you anything that is not going forward is going out . . . You know what we can do with special effects and electric brain stimulation . . . Some joker gets out of line we press a button and he shits in his pants at sight of her. That at least would be a step in some direction . . ."

"For Godsake not at this point. If the Queen tries to grab more than she's got imagewise she will lose it all . . . uh I mean we will . . . All the others are hopeless . . . Any of you jokers like to try propping up the queen of Denmark? I say leave it just where it is. It will stagger on for another five or ten years and that's enough. We get smart at this point and the English Republican Party will jump out at us . . ."

ERP ERP ERP:

"The Queen is an alien symbol basically Germanic in Origin. The Queen is also a *white* symbol. The White Goddess in fact. Young people want that? Black people want that? Who wants a grovel symbol? Those who need such symbols to keep positions of wealth and privilege. Look at them. Look at Jennifer's Diary . . ."

"I mean ERP could be dangerous."

"That's right. We got a good strong thing here why muck about with it?"

"Why the whole stinking thing could blow up in our faces . . ."

"Brings on my ulcers to think about it . . ."

"We could organize ERP . . ."

"That way we'd be ready to jump in either direction . . ."

"The word that made a man out of an ape and killed the ape in the process keeps man an animal the way we like to see him. And the Queen is just another prop to hold up the word. You all know what we can do with the word. Talk about the power in an atom. All hate all fear all pain all death all sex is in the word. The word was a killer virus once. It could become a killer virus again. The word is too hot to handle so we sit on our ass waiting for the pension. But somebody is going to pick up that virus and use it . . . *Virus B-23* . . .''

"Aw we got the Shines cooled back with Che Guevara in a 19th-century set . . .''

"Is that right? And you got the Tiddlywinks cooled too? You can cool anybody else who gets ideas? You going to cool this powder keg with your moth-eaten Queen? I tell you anybody could turn it loose. You all know how basically simple it is . . . Sex word and image cut in with death word and image . . .''

"Yeah *we* could do it."

"But what about Washington? Our orders?"

"Just one test tube and SPUT . . . What Washington? What orders?"

FROM HERE TO ETERNITY

Mildred Pierce reporting:

I was there. I saw it. I saw women thrown down on Fifth Avenue and raped in their mink coats by blacks and whites and yellows while street urchins stripped the rings from their fingers. A young officer stood nearby.

"Aren't you going to DO something?" I demanded.

He looked at me and yawned.

I found Colonel Bradshaw bivouacking in the Ritz. I told him bluntly what was going on. His eyes glinted shamelessly as he said: "Well you have to take a broad general view of things."

And that's what I have been doing. Taking a broad general view of American troops raping and murdering helpless civilians while American officers stand around and yawn.

"Been at it a long time, lady. It's the old army game from here to eternity."

This license was dictated by considerations taken into account by prudent commanders throughout history. It pays to pay the boys off. Even the noble Brutus did it . . .

Points with his left hand in catatonic limestone . . .
"The town is yours soldier brave."

Tacitus describes a typical scene . . . "If a woman
or a good-looking boy fell into their hands they were
torn to pieces in the struggle for possession and the
survivors were left to cut each other's throats."

"Well there's no need to be that messy. Why waste
a good-looking boy? Mother-loving American Army
run by old women many of them religious my God
hanging American soldiers for raping and murdering
civilians . . ."

Old Sarge bellows from here to eternity
"WHAT THE BLOODY FUCKING HELL ARE
CIVILIANS FOR? *SOLDIERS PAY.*"

The CO stands there and smiles. Just ahead is a
middle-western town on a river 30,000 civilians. The
CO points:

"It's all yours boys. Every man woman and child.
God is nigh."

"LET'S GET US SOME CIVIES."

"Now just a minute boys listen to Old Sarge. Why
make the usual stupid scene kicking in liquor stores
grabbing anything in sight? You wake up hung-over
in an alley your prick sore from fucking dry cunts and
assholes your eye gouged out by a broken beer bottle
you and your asshole buddy wanted the same piece of
ass. No fun in that. Why not leave it like this? They go
about their daily tasks and we just take what we want
when we want it cool and steady easy and make them
like it. You see what I mean."

The young lieutenant from camouflage sees what he

means . . . BOYS . . . swimming pools and locker rooms full of them.

"Getting it steady year after year. Now that's what I call PAY."

Precarious governments march in anywhere and take over . . . war lords . . . city states fortified against foraging crowds from the starving cities . . . power cut . . . reservoirs blown up . . .

Crowds are looting the museums for weapons . . . Stone axes, Fijian war clubs, Samurai swords, crossbows, bolos, boomerangs . . . They put on costumes to match. Militant queens snatch up krises . . . "LET'S RUN AMOK DUCKS IT'S FUN." . . . They hit the street in loincloths.

Drunken Yale boys put on armor and charge down Fifth Avenue on horseback skewering the passers-by.

A World War I tank with cheering doughboys is driven off a museum pedestal.

The militants raid government laboratories. Virus B-23 rages through cities of the world like a topping forest fire. In the glow of burning cities strange cults spring up.

The Vigilantes sweep up from the Bible Belt like a plague of locusts hanging every living thing in their path. Even horses are hauled into the air kicking and farting.

The dreaded Baseball Team 5000 burly athletes in baseball uniforms all with special bats erupt into a crowded street . . .

"BEAT YOUR FILTHY BRAINS OUT . . ."

Smashing shop windows blood brains and broken glass in their wake . . .

The Chinese waiters charge with meat cleavers . . .
"FLUCK YOU FLUCK YOU FLUCK YOU . . ."

In ruined suburbs naked bacchantes chase a scream-ing boy. Now the roller-skate boys sweep down a hill on jet skates in a shower of blue sparks and cut the bacchantes to pieces with their 18-inch bowie knives. The new boy is issued a knife and skates. Splashed with blood from head to foot they jet away singing

"FOR EVERY MASS MURDER LET US STAND PREPARED."

THE TEACHER

Vista of riots and burning cities cuts to a remote muted board room. Faces of wealth and power sipping ice water. A padded door flies open in a blast of riot sound effects Audrey Carsons in a light black suit and grey fedora dances into the board room with Charlie Workman and Jimmy the Shrew.

"I'm the Sheik of Araby . . ."

He shatters a pitcher of ice water on the table grabs the chairman by the tie holding the jagged shards inches from his face.

"Or else belongs to me . . ."

The board members disappear in a silver flash. Weary old voice drifts from a tape recorder.

"Smeared with the blood of old movies we hope to last?"

"The song is ended . . ."

Audrey points to the night sky over St Louis Missouri the old broken point of origin. A cluster of stars winks out.

"Dead stars. We went out long ago."

"But the melody lingers on . . ."

Darkness falls on beer drops and Harlem streets.

"Now you and the song are gone . . ."

"Or else come and took over."

"But the melody lingers on . . ."

Public school classroom 1920s. Albert Stern as the teacher is calling the roll.

"Arthur Flegenheimer . . ."

Camera pans through corridors and dining room grey sugar greasy black cutlery.

"Arthur Flegenheimer . . ."

Camera tracks through washrooms and toilets.

Come and jack off . . . June 17, 1922.

Phallic shadows on a distant wall.

"Arthur Flegenheimer . . ."

The teacher writes Absent by his name.

The screen darkens into the hiss of a gas oven and hospital sound effects.

Newspaper picture of the waxen corpse of Albert Stern looking like the little man on a wedding cake.

GANG "KILLER" A SUICIDE IN RAGS.

Newspaper picture of Dutch Schultz on deathbed.

DUTCH SCHULTZ DEAD.

On the day that Dutch Schultz died the winning number was 00. His number was up.

Harlem basement cabaret. . . music. . . lights. . . a faggot prances out in a pea-green suit and grey fedora.

ARTIST

"COME IN WITH THE DUTCHMAN
COME IN WITH THE DUTCHMAN
COME IN WITH THE DUTCHMAN
OR ELSE"

He clutches his chest and does a split pratfall. The hat flies off his head on spring. He zips his legs together and catches the hat.

"COME IN WITH THE DUTCHMAN
COME IN WITH THE DUTCHMAN
COME IN WITH THE DUTCHMAN
OR ELSE"

He smashes a bag of ketchup against his face, grabs his crotch and bends forward wiggling his ass like a randy dog.

CLUB 400 . . . Chauffeur-driven limousines guests in evening dress bowed in by the obsequious snarling doorman.

"Good evening Mr Poindexter . . ."

"BEAT IT YOU FUCKING BUM."

A moving van stops in front of the 400 and a pack of yelping screaming faggots leap out led by the ARTIST. They buzz by the doorman one snatches his hat and fill the club screeching, camping, snatching table-cloths curtains and drapes for impersonation acts. The ARTIST jumps up onto the bar and does The Strip Polka.

"TAKE IT OFF TAKE IT OFF
SCREAM THE GIRLS FROM THE REAR"

Woman is helped into her mink coat by hat-check girl. She preens herself then sniffs and stiffens and looks down. Her coat is in rags steaming red and orange fumes blobs of smoking fur fall to the floor. She screams like a baby.

Cry of new-born baby . . . a door opens . . . Doctor Stern thin, tubercular, sad stands in the doorway.

"You can come in now Mr Flegenheimer . . . a fine boy . . . where can I wash my hands?"

Dutch washing his hands in the lavatory of THE PALACE CHOP HOUSE. The door opens behind him. Sound and smell of frying steak.

Hospital sound effects hospital room. Dutch in bed two detectives and a police stenographer with clipboard.

1ST DETECTIVE
"Who shot you?"
DUTCH
"I don't know sir honestly I don't. I went to the toilet. I was in the toilet and when I reached the (a word not clear) the boy came at me."

Police stenographer writes this down.

2ND DETECTIVE
"What boy?"

Dutch as youth in street crap game. He has thrown a seven but the dice are still moving as a boy snatches them up.

BOY
"THEY'RE MY DICE."
DUTCH
"How much did you have in the pot?"
BOY
"Not a nickle."

Dutch kicks him in the mouth knocking out his front teeth. Flash of the boy's shocked bleeding face.

Cut back to the teacher calling the roll in Public School 12 1922.

TEACHER
"Arthur Flegenheimer . . ."

Dutch clutches his side in the lavatory of THE PALACE CHOP HOUSE.

DUTCH
"OH MAMA MAMA I BEEN SHOT THROUGH THE LIVER."
1ST DETECTIVE
"Don't holler."
DUTCH
"Mother is the best bet and don't let Satan draw you too fast."
2ND DETECTIVE
"Now what are we sitting here for?"
DUTCH
"In the olden days they waited and they waited."
1ST DETECTIVE
"Don't get wise."

Hospital room some hours later. There is only one detective in the room and he is dozing in a chair. Grey immobile the SCRIBE looks down at his clipboard pencil poised waiting. Dutch speaks in the voice of Albert Stern.

ALBERT STERN
"Please let me get in and eat."

Police stenographer writes this down. Detective wakes up.

DETECTIVE
"Who shot you?"
DUTCH
"The boss himself."

THE SILVER CORD an exclusive night club. The proprietor is seen unhooking the famous silver rope to admit favored clients. Albert Stern in a filthy evening jacket pocked with cigarette burns his pants held up by a length of rope runs toward the silver cord the doorman ten feet behind him.

ALBERT STERN
"PLEASE LET ME GET IN AND EAT."

Behind the doorman is a flying wedge of panhandlers. They burst through the cord ripping it from the hook.

DUTCH
"Oh mama mama DON'T TEAR DON'T RIP . . ."
1ST DETECTIVE
"Control yourself."

They pour into the dining room. The waiters try to oust them but they are like sacks of mendicant concrete clutching at the guests with filthy fingers, snatching food and drinks from the tables, urinating on the floor.

Death pees with decayed fingers. The Dutchman washes his hands.

A flashy overexpensive night spot. Officious waiters with a flourish deposit dishes with a silver cover on tables.

WAITER 1

"Voilà le *Lapin Chasseur* . . ."

He lifts the cover to reveal the bloated corpse of a huge rat showing its yellow teeth in a pile of garbage.

WAITER 2

"Voilà le *Faisan Suprême* . . ."

Lifts cover to reveal a buzzard cooked in sewage.

WAITER 3

"Voilà les *Fruits de Mer* . . ."

Lifts cover to reveal a live horseshoe crab on its back in used condoms shit-stained newspapers and bloody Kotex.

The guests scream gag cover their faces with napkins.

Room in OLD HARMONY HOTEL upstate New York red curtains and carpets turn-of-the-century décor DEATH OF STONEWALL JACKSON on the wall.

"That picture's awful dusty . . ."

Dixie Davis is reading *Collier's* magazine. Martin Krompier looks at the ceiling. They are both very bored with the argument between Dutch and Jules Martin.

DUTCH

"I don't want harmony. I want harmony. Oh mama mama who give it to him?"

1ST DETECTIVE

"Who give it to *you* Dutch?"

Dutch pours a drink and shoves his face within inches of Martin's.

DUTCH

"So Jules Judas Martin thought the Dutchman was through did he? Thought he could put his big greasy mitt in for forty thousand clams did he?"

JULES MARTIN

"Look Dutch we don't owe a nickle . . ."

DUTCH

"Cut that out we don't owe a nickle . . ."

JULES MARTIN

"SAY LIST . . ."

DUTCH

"Shut up you gotta big mouth . . ."

As he says this Dutch flips a .38 from his waistband shoves the barrel right into Martin's mouth and pulls the trigger. Jules Martin falls to the floor screaming moaning spitting blood and smoke.

In the hospital room doctor is filing the end off morphine ampoule and filling syringe.

1ST DETECTIVE

"Can't you give him something that will get him to talk doctor?"

DOCTOR

"Talk to *who?* The man is delirious . . ."

DUTCH

"Oh and then he clips me . . . Come on cut that out we don't owe a nickle . . ."

JULES MARTIN

"SAY LIST . . ."

1ST DETECTIVE

"WHAT are you? a ventriloquist?"

2ND DETECTIVE
"Control yourself."

Dixie Davis snatches up his coat and briefcase and flounces to the door. With his hand on the brass doorknob he turns around.

DIXIE DAVIS
"To do a thing like that right in front of me Arthur . . . After all I'm a professional man . . ."

He opens the door. Hotel porter walks by whistling "Home Sweet Home" down the empty corridor.

DUTCH
"A boy has never wept or dashed a thousand Kim."
1ST DETECTIVE
"That takes the rag off the bush."

The SCRIBE writes boys running and beckoning from playgrounds and bridges. A skull-faced porter turns around. The number on his cap is 23.

TEACHER
"Arthur Flegenheimer . . ."
2ND DETECTIVE
"Was it the boss shot you?"
1ST DETECTIVE
(Wheedling and obscene) "Come on Dutch who shot you?"
2ND DETECTIVE
(Tough and peremptory) "Come on Dutch who shot you?"

Campaign poster of the DA his mustache bristling

ominously dissolves to 12 men seated at long table. Background shots vaguely seen are taken from other sets in the film. This is the board room, the hospital room, Dutch's office, THE PALACE CHOP HOUSE. At one end of the table sits an old Don with dark glasses. At the other end sits Lepke Buchalter the JUDGE doe-eyed and enigmatic. He is the nominal chairman but the old Don is obviously in control.

OLD DON
"Kick him upstairs into a governor . . ."

ANASTASIA
"Or President even . . ."

MEMBER 3
"DAs come and go . . ."

GURRAH
"Why wait? I say hit him . . ."

MEMBER 5
"We can ride this out. I say forget him . . ."

LUCKY LUCIANO
"This is 1935 not 1925. Time to pack in the cowboy act."

MEMBER 8
"Brings on my ulcers to think about it."

MEMBER 9
"Undecided."

DUTCH
"I say he's got to be hit on the head. We gotta make an example."

JUDGE
"An example of what Mr Flegenheimer? There seems to be a difference of opinion. We will put it to a vote

. . . for or against?" . . . (He glances at the old Don)
. . . "My vote is against."

OLD DON

(Shakes his head and smiles) "Against."

ANASTASIA

(He lifts his hands and turns them out) . . . "It's a
natural It's beautiful . . . but . . ."
(He drops his hands palm down on the table)
"Against."

LUCKY LUCIANO

"Against."

MEMBER 8

"Against it from the beginning."

MEMBER 9

"I'm against it."

MEMBER 5

"Against."

DUTCH

"Wait a minute here . . ."

JUDGE

"You are outvoted Mr Flegenheimer."

DUTCH

"He's gotta go. If no one else is gonna do it I'm gonna
hit him myself."

The old Don smiles . . . hospital sound effects . . .
voice of nurse echoes down the hall . . .

NURSE

"Quarter grain GOM . . ."

Car in Holland Tunnel. Piggy is at the wheel his
round pale face smooth and bland. The hulking snarl-

ing strangler Mendy Weiss sits on the jump seat. In the back seat are Charlie The Bug Workman and Jimmy the Shrew. Workman is a cool casual killer in a tailor-made twilight blue suit and grey fedora pale face cold metallic grey eyes. The Shrew is in the tight pea-green suit and grey fedora smooth poreless red skin tight over the cheekbones lips parted from long yellow teeth the color of old ivory. The tunnel lights ring their heads with an orange halo.

ARTIST
"COME IN WITH THE DUTCHMAN
COME IN WITH THE DUTCHMAN
COME IN WITH THE DUTCHMAN"

Back room of THE PALACE CHOP HOUSE. Dutch is sitting at a table with Lulu Rosencrantz, Abe Landau and Otto Daba Berman. Beer mugs on the table cigar smoking in an ash tray. Aba Daba is working adding machine and writing figures down on ledger paper.

DUTCH
"HEY WONG."

Chinese cook appears in upper panel of green door leading to the kitchen.

"Steak medium with French fries."

The cook nods and disappears.
Press conference the Police Commissioner behind his desk.

REPORTER
"Any line on the Dutch Schultz shoot-down Commissioner?"

COMMISSIONER

"We have. At least one of the gunmen has been positively identified as Albert Stern.

REPORTER

"Who's this Albert Stern?"

COMMISSIONER

"Because of his spectacles and his mild appearance he is known as the Teacher. Wild Boy would be a better name for him. A hophead gunman top trigger for the Big Six he is probably one of the most dangerous killers alive today.

Hospital room. Detectives are drinking coffee from paper cups.

DUTCH

"Come on open the soap duckets."

Sound of frying fat.

Flash of city after nuclear attack . . . rubble . . . heat waves . . . a gang of boys carrying shards and bars of blistered metal . . . faces of hatred evil and despair streaked with coal dust.

DUTCH

"THE CHIMNEY SWEEPS TAKE TO THE SWORD . . ."

2ND DETECTIVE

"The doctor wants you to lie quiet."

Porter whistles "Home Sweet Home" down the corridor of OLD HARMONY HOTEL.

Color shot of advertisement circa 1910 shows blown-up soup tin. Written on it in rainbow letters RAINBOW JACK'S FRENCH CANADIAN BEAN SOUP. Picture on can shows mountain lake and rainbow red-haired lumber-jack holds up the can with the picture on it.

DUTCH
"French Canadian Bean Soup . . ."

Bare room of Albert Stern. He is lying by the open gas oven. Hiss of escaping gas mixes with hospital sound effects.

DUTCH
"I want to pay. Let them leave me alone."

Teacher calling the roll in Public School 12. This shot rapidly darkens.

TEACHER
"Arthur Flegenheimer
Arthur Flegenheimer."

A last despairing cry from darkness.

"ARTHUR FLEGENHEIMER . . ."

Darkness on screen. Silence on screen.

THEY DO NOT ALWAYS REMEMBER

It was in Monterrey Mexico . . . a square a fountain a café. I had stopped by the fountain to make an entry in my notebook: "dry fountain empty square silver paper in the wind frayed sounds of a distant city."

"What have you written there?" I looked up. A man was standing in front of me barring the way. He was corpulent but hard-looking with a scarred red face and pale grey eyes. He held out his hand as if presenting a badge but the hand was empty. In the same movement he took the notebook out of my hands.

"You have no right to do that. What I write in a notebook is my business. Besides I don't believe you are a police officer."

Several yards away I saw a uniformed policeman thumbs hooked in his belt. "Let's see what he has to say about this."

We walked over to the policeman. The man who had stopped me spoke rapidly in Spanish and handed him the notebook. The policeman leafed through it. I was about to renew my protests but the policeman's manner was calm and reassuring. He handed the notebook back to me said something to the other man who went back and stood by the fountain.

"You have time for a coffee *señor?*" the policeman asked. "I will tell you a story. Years ago in this city there were two policemen who were friends and shared the same lodgings. One was Rodriguez. He was content to be a simple *agente* as you see me now. The other was Alfaro. He was brilliant, ambitious and rose rapidly in the force until he was second in command. He introduced new methods . . . tape recorders . . . speech prints. He even studied telepathy and took a drug once which he thought would enable him to detect the criminal mind. He did not hesitate to take action where more discreet officials preferred to look the other way . . . the opium fields . . . the management of public funds . . . bribery in the police force . . . the behavior of policemen off-duty. *Señor* he put through a rule that any police officer drunk and carrying a pistol would have his pistol permit canceled for one flat year and what is more he enforced the rule. Needless to say he made enemies. One night he received a phone call and left the apartment he still shared with Rodriguez . . . he had never married and preferred to live simply you understand . . . just there by the fountain he was struck by a car . . . an accident? perhaps . . . for months he lay in a coma between life and death . . . he recovered finally . . . perhaps it would have been better if he had not." The policeman tapped his forehead "You see the brain was damaged . . . a small pension . . . he still thinks he is a major of police and sometimes the old Alfaro is there. I recall an American tourist, cameras slung all over him like great tits protesting waving his passport. There he made a mistake. I looked at the passport and did not like what I saw. So I took him along to the *comisaria* where it came to light the passport was forged the American tourist was a Dane wanted for passing worthless checks in twenty-three countries including Mexico. A female impersonator from East St Louis turned out to be an atomic scientist wanted by the FBI for selling secrets to the Chinese. Yes thanks to Alfaro I have made important arrests. More often I must tell to some tourist once again the story of Rodriguez and Alfaro." He took a toothpick out of his mouth and looked meditatively at the end of it. "I think Rodriguez has his Alfaro and for every Alfaro there is always a Rodriguez. They do not always remember." He tapped his forehead. "You will pay the coffee yes?"

I put a note down on the table. Rodriguez snatched it up. "This note is counterfeit *señor*. You are under arrest." "But I got it from American Express two hours ago!" "*Mentiras!* You think we Mexicans are so stupid? No doubt you have a suitcase full of this filth in your hotel room." Alfaro was standing by the table smiling. He showed a police badge. "I am the FBI *señor* . . . the Federal Police of Mexico. Allow me." He took the note and held it up to the light smiling he handed it back to me. He said something to Rodriguez who walked out and stood by the fountain. I noticed for the first time that he was not carrying a pistol. Alfaro looked after him shaking his head sadly. "You have time for a coffee *señor?* I will tell you a story." "That's enough!" I pulled a card out of my wallet and snapped crisply "I am District Supervisor Lee of the American Narcotics Department and I am arresting you and your accomplice Rodriguez for acting in concert to promote the sale of narcotics . . . caffeine among other drugs . . .''

A hand touched my shoulder. I looked up. A grey-haired Irishman was standing there with calm authority the face portentous and distant as if I were recovering consciousness after a blow on the head. They do not always remember. ''Go over there by the fountain Bill. I'll look into this.'' I could feel his eyes on my back see the sad head shake hear him order two coffees in excellent Spanish . . . dry fountain empty square silver paper in the wind frayed sounds of distant city . . . everything grey and fuzzy . . . my mind isn't working right . . . who are you over there telling the story of Harry and Bill? . . . The square clicked back into focus. My mind cleared. I walked toward the café with calm authority.

FRIENDS

I had a good steady trade built up of commuters and office people no trouble from this crowd they were all being psychoanalyzed which takes all the fight out of a man but sometimes they got maudlin and the analyst earns his money hearing about it the next day. I was putting it aside for a spaceship I was building on my Missouri farm I needed a few more parts, expensive parts. I've always had a knack for bartending which is I hate the customer and treat him with great courtesy and they think I'm the greatest guy in the world and every night at commuters time a respectful mutter goes up and down the bar

"Johnny is a great guy."

"My favorite bartender" trills a sex-change case who was one of my steadies and brought in a lot of trade she was a *character* and commuters love them. I've had a lot of these characters in my place with monkeys and dogs and mongooses that drink cocktails or some of them eat razor blades. Only one I ever barred out was a bastard with an 18-inch centipede he would suddenly flip out in your face. I brought my snub-nosed .38 up slow you can see the bullet at the end of the barrel and I said

"Get out of here with that fucking thing or I'll kill you."

But mostly they're harmless you know I'll jump over a walking stick held in both hands and remove my vest without removing my coat. I was about to sell the place and buy the parts I needed and on my way rejoicing my God what a planet of slobs when what should walk into my place but this Clancy the cop with his buckles and badge all shiny a big smile on his face and cold twinkling blue eyes like sunlight on ice. I didn't like to see him in my place and I could see all the commuters huddling together for comfort like the wise monkeys. I took my time serving him and when I did I walked over slow and said

"What'll you have mister?"

"You can call me Clancy" he said smiling as if this was a great joke. I didn't think it was funny.

"What'll you have Clancy" I said deadpan.

"Budweiser."

I served him he takes a deep drag and looks around. Nobody met his eyes but he catches one of them looking away and says "Howdy" smiling away.

"Uh good evening huhump."

Then Clancy walks over and lays a hand on his shoulder . . . "I can see you're clean and decent so you shouldn't be nervous talking to a cop . . . You got a light?"

The commuter's hand was shaking so he had to steady it with the other hand clasped around his wrist to light Clancy's cigarette while Clancy just looks at him and smiles.

"Uh I haveta make a train . . ."

"The next train doesn't leave for twenty minutes so there's time for you to have a drink on me. Always time for that right friend?"

"Oh uh yeah thanks."

"Well drink up. And if there's one thing I'm sure of it's that you and I are *friends*. Come in here every night do you?"

Next night Clancy was my only customer. I slapped his beer in front of him.

"Well now you seem kinda pissed about something Marty."

"You drive out my customers when I'm trying to sell the joint . . . How can I sell a bar with nothing but one cop in it anybody walks in on a scene like that needs his head examined."

"Well now maybe I could bring you the cop trade."

"Who'd buy a barful of you bastards getting drunk and shooting the bartender?"

I had my magnetic shield up. I wasn't afraid of anything he could do. At a certain level you understand there are certain things which anyone reaching that level may be presumed to know. Undoubtedly they'd been over my equipment I never really learn to *write* this earth language went to a progressive school you understand we all had to be *borned* here as humans I would never be a volunteer again for such an assignment like I could hear Clancy's report

"Old fashioned time equipment workable to be sure. The only weaponry seems to be a primitive laser installation."

"So you figure there's no danger Clancy?"

"I didn't say that sir. In fact it worries me sir."

"I thought he was your *friend* Clancy."

"So did I sir" said Clancy unhappily. There was something about the man a furtiveness of person and motive after all where was he escaping to? *Who* was he escaping to? Some hidden *friend?* Who was he? Could it be that he didn't need *friends?*

"Clancy I know one thing. I have no enemies. I turn them all into *friends* one way or another."

SEEING RED

Arriving at customs Lee is ushered to the special shed where nine agents wait.

"Let's see what this dirty writer is trying to smuggle through decent American customs . . ."

The agent with one arm reaches all the way to the bottom of the wickerwork suitcase and pulls out the Picture . . . room with rose wallpaper bathed in a smoky sunset on a brass bed a red-haired boy with a hard-on sprawls one bare knee flopped against the greasy pink wallpaper he is playing a flute and looking at somebody standing in front of the picture. The agent stares and the red picture turns his face to flame. He makes a slight choking sound and looks helplessly at his fellow agents who look back dumb stricken faces swollen with blood. None of them can articulate a word. The agent stands there holding the picture looking from the picture to angry red faces as more and more agents crowd into the shed. No one looks at Lee. He closes his bags, hails an old junkie porter and leaves the shed. Behind him a ripping splintering crash as the walls of the shed give way.

Outside the pier prowl cars converge like electric

turtles disgorging load after load of flushed cops. Silent catatonic they crowd around the picture looking at each other the agent there holding the picture up like a banner of raw meat suddenly two jets of blood spurt from his eyes. Silently he proffers the picture to a fellow agent and sinks to the boards of the pier. A choking red haze steams from the purple faces. There is an occasional muffled report as blood vessels burst and sinuses explode. Wave after wave of silent cops crowd onto the pier which sags and finally gives way with a crash that host of cops sink like lead into the sea.

The picture in its rosewood frame floats there on the green water looking up at the sky and the cops keep coming. Texas Rangers with huge Magnum revolvers and pale nigger-killing eyes. The Royal Mounted faces as red as their uniforms.

The picture floats there in the green water where all plunge and perish . . .

The Piper pulled down the sky.

OLD MOVIE

In the noon streets three men sitting on ash cans. One of the men looked up and saw Agent 23. Electric hate crackled between them. In a panic 23 tried to pull his eyes back. He could not do so. He held one point and felt the pilot land. Something cracked in his head like a red egg and the ground swayed beneath him then he could feel it pouring out his eyes. A crowd was gathering quick and silent eyes blazing hate. 23 ran toward them up the narrow street moving his head from side to side burning a path through charred flesh and shredded brains running very light on his feet up the steep stone street toward the skies of Marrakech the whole film tilted now the stones moving in waves under his feet a blaze of blue and he was stabbing two black holes in the blue sky smoking with a sound like falling mountains the sky ripped open and he was through the film barrier. Standing naked in front of a washstand copper luster basin the film jumped and shifted music across the golf course he was a caddy it seems looking for lost balls by the pond flickering silver buttocks in the dark room fading flickering all from an old movie that will give at his touch.

ELECTRICALS

"The old lady was getting ready to have me put away for shock treatment they were big tough come along sonny slobs three of them caught in slow motion I was that much faster turning his stupid face right into my elbow when I 'let self go.' (The karate instructor told me: ' "Let self go" come when you need it like bolt of lightning. Pick up bolt and use it.') Breaking bones with every kick cartilages crunch kidneys rupture under my chops and knees and elbows a Lindy Hop in broken bones I can feel my eyes light up inside grab his sap and beat his brains out. I put on my roller skates and glide away into the summer night I can see in the dark. Seeing my eyes in the dark they would say 'Oh a cat or some other animal undoubtedly harmless.' We can see their slower reflexes and slower minds spread out like a map and plot our course I saw his eyes and found the boy in darkness sitting on the stone bridge no one ventures down along the dark footpaths under the dripping trees sluggish streams and swamps snakes too we can always find a spot where they won't be and move from spot to spot seeing someone in the dark is like a take from a pinhole camera dim and grainy we live in darkness just out of their sight in the sounds they cannot hear in the colors they cannot see where they are not we are grey shadows across the boy's shirt the racing clouds the pools of darkness.''

Jimmy Catfield had always been a shy quiet boy but he had a murderous temper. A loud-mouthed school bully went to the hospital when he picked Jimmy up by the back of his coat and said ''Look the little fairy can fly.'' Jimmy twisted around quick as a weasel and broke his jaw with a hammer chop. One night five townies laid for him under the railroad bridge older taller heavier waiting there the druggist's son Guy Macintosh, the ferret-faced boy from Doc's pool room —Jimmy once saw him use a broken bottle on a drunk's face—leather-jacket boy bicycle chain dangling from his red fish fist, the sheriff's son with dad's sap which he handles obscenely and the fat degenerate boy who worked in Ma Green's florist shop. Jimmy felt his hair stand up and his eyes light up inside and he charged taking them by surprise. A quick chop to the wrist and he had the bicycle chain swinging it over his head danced and whirled cutting faces to the bone knees and elbows crunching deadly will-o'-the-wisp one lay dead his throat ripped out. Two others would be in hospital for some time. The sheriff's son and the florist boy took to their heels like panicked elephants splashing through the swamp. The florist boy went down in quicksand screaming for the Blessed Virgin. The sheriff's son staggered back to town clothes ripped to shreds by brambles.

''Pull yourself together son what happened?''

"We were wiped out Ma. He ain't human. My buddy's out there with his throat ripped open to the spine I seen it cut him like a buzz saw not a cop's son for nothing I know when to run and the way Stinky went down screaming for the Virgin to Jesus hope I never see a sight like that again sand sucking him in like a great big . . . aw gee Ma I almost said a dirty word like a big rectum mother I'm all in. I need one of your Miltowns."

"Of course you poor boy better take two." She picked up the phone. "And as for that Catfield brat . . ."

One late afternoon Peter looked across the roofs of the city he began to walk the roofs leaping across gangways from tree to window ledge against the violet evening sky he could fly almost. A policeman's bullet put him in a wheel chair . . . Ward 23 . . . We were there to forget this nonsense with the flying the fighting the seeing in the dark the balancing too gut the jumping too far the kindly German psychiatrist told us. We have a plan called Demolition 23. Operation entails staying conscious during shock therapy. Control tells us this can activate a death ray from the eyes. So we can kill the nurses, attendants, doctors and above all the vile cooks in that hospital. General instructions relax muscles and let current flow through like water. Messages passed along in muscle talk years of knowledge from a twitching cheek calf thigh legends of the ward: The Music Box Twins who could squeak out "The Last Roundup" when they turned the juice through them. Willy the Grounder. The current ran around him right down the bedpost electrocuted the head matron who had rushed in with wet galoshes she did a Lindy Hop and sizzled. Willy got so he could store it like an eel. There was a crackling blue halo round his body smell of ozone. And he grounded all the grills and keys drains and radiators no place he couldn't ground them waiter spills water on their feet wind whips a fountain cross the path good doctor relaxing in his bath bites his cigar in two turns red as a lobster and his eyes pop out.

Brad was taking a shower and Greg sat in the living room petulantly leafing through *The New Yorker* it isn't *funny* any more he was horrified to see Brad burst from the shower stark naked doing an obscene dance with a crackling hula-hoop trailing a fine wire it was Brad's passion to hula-hoop under the shower. In a flash Greg snatched up a wire cutter and snipped the wire Brad fell to the floor in a heavy swoon. Greg gave him the kiss of life then he was breathing his body outlined in blue fire and Greg knew he was an *electrical* with a lithe movement twisted Reg on all fours they streak away through the sky and come the milky way.

Now I was an exponent of the activist school. Ride the charge like bucking white hot wire dance it jump it stay ahead of it when the current hits I feel my hair stand on end the mouth plug flies out I break the strap and sit up current blazing out my eyes spitting death. They scream and claw at empty eye sockets smolder and lay still. I slip out of bed examine the doctor the nurse the technician. They are dead hair burning.

I went back to the ward and rigged the boys with battery sets. Peter was the first to "get his eyes."

Whipping along in his wheel chair when a Lesbian nurse we called her Our Lady of Lourdes barred his way. "Now where do you think you're going young man?" He turns on the juice and burns her down hot brains spatter the wall like the powdered scrambled eggs they serve us, and in that moment he found he could walk. We clean out the hospital and all the boys get their eyes and we have eyes for the kindly German psychiatrist. He holds up his hands. "Tell me what grievance you got Jungen." We tell him and he falls smoking full of holes. And now for those fucking cooks.

SPUT

After that we were on the run never staying more than one night in the same hotel, the Dib was coughing and sweating at night and he had nightmares and when he woke up he would sob into the pillow

"Johnny we gotta get *out* of here . . . Don't let me die here . . ."

One night we checked into a hotel late I didn't like the looks of the clerk a fattish man with cold eyes he took our money and shoved the key at us. When we got to room 23 we both stripped we were hot after three days in the street the Dib got down on all fours and slapped his thighs

"Asi Johnny."

I got down on all fours in front of him facing the wardrobe mirror and the door the Walther with silencer on the bed right by my hand the Dib behind me we were twisting in the tarnished mirror silver buttocks feeling the squeeze in my nuts when there was a key in the lock and two plainclothes dicks burst in the clerk behind them. I saw the Dib's hair stand up on end and then my hand found the Walther they were vice squad cops and it took them by surprise one of

them had pop brown eyes nearly jumped out on the
floor when he saw us like that then my hand found
the Walther and he did a double take and reached for
his gun in a hip holster his vest pulled up showing a
patch of white shirt

SPUT

There was a splash of red and he sagged just as
the gun jumped in my hand I went off and I was still
spurting as I pivoted and got the other dick right in
the mouth the Dib got the clerk and he went down
like a sack of concrete the room was full of the smell
of cordite sperm and rectal mucus smoke drifting
back across our faces in the shooting the Dib had
come too and his dick was still throbbing in my ass.
We pulled them inside and closed the door got dressed
and out of there fast hung a DO NOT DISTURB sign on
the door . . .

There didn't seem to be any way out we were caught
there in our dead flesh. The Dib was spitting blood
now and his breath was sour. One night we found ourselves wandering around in the snow. We had lost our
guns somehow I don't remember staggering around
in the snow filthy unshaven and then I saw the police
kiosk ahead. It was on the outskirts about ten cops
frisking some young hoodlums and the photographers
ready. No chance to turn back they'd seen us I had
one grenade left. I tossed the grenade into the air
above their heads

SPUT . . . an explosion of darkness.

Virus B-23 opened a Pandora box of biologic and
chemical weapons . . .

delicate youths spotted with decay like a ripe peach
diseased ravening vampire face torn with hideous
    hungers
farts and belches from unknown foods
shrill siren songs and slimy evil whispers that stick
    in the throat
words you can smell giggling out the plague

The intense displaced misery of those years is reflected in the rainbow. Musky red trip but we are here flesh steaming red a human ass farts light. Empty house and wall. Glad tidings for Control.

REDDIES

From Jerry the red wolfboy sprang the Reddies semi-hermaphrodites who undergo biologic change during intercourse . . .

"Step right up ladies and gentlemen and bring your cats and dogs goats and monkeys with such hair too the Big Store is open. You have only to pay the price . . . The biologic price you understand"

Curtain parts on a room with rose wallpaper where two naked red-haired boys stand looking at each other like tomcats. They turn redder bodies blushing cocks sway and stiffen a musky fox smell fills the room and drifts out on the hot still summer afternoon

Scattered coughs from the audience . . . screams of rage and protest

One boy's face gathers reptilian force. His nipples disappear in swirls of nitrous vapor leaving two pearly disks . . . loud snap . . . crackling sounds . . .

"Now some of you may have noticed a strange odor that emanates from these characters . . . a sweet rotten musky nitrous ozone smell like a den of randy foxes in a photographic darkroom . . . whiffs of cyanide coal gas and carrion . . ."

The other boy turns bright red sways dizzily his face torn by naked lust and pain nitrous vapors steam off him his nipples swell to the size of a peach spotted with purple bruises erect quivering as a pearly tentacle from the other boy's navel wraps around him he falls on the bed. The tentacle pulls the other boy on the bed in a quick leap he shoves the boy's legs apart the rectum a pink quivering ring lined with a soft mucilage like red frog eggs and the smell reeks out of him . . .

"It acts like cyanide on a tight white RIGHTIE anybody who *has to be right* because it moves the biologic position and that character is now WRONG . . ."

Nigger-killing lawmen, decent church-going women turn blue and flop around in their shit . . . A little boy looks at them severely and says . . . "Take them outside because they stink."

"Now children generally like this smell and come out in red itchy blotches that feel good when they scratch and say . . . "Geeeee you can keep me here as long as you like as long as you give me *these* . . ."

Adolescent stands with his fly sticking out and the pimples explode all over his face . . .

"Young boys need it special."

He looks at his friend and they are taking off their pants the boys are coming now teeth bare eyes burning bright green and yellow the hair bristles and stirs all over their bodies sprouts into red animal hair . . . canines tear through bleeding gums . . . the smell attracts all delicate and furtive animals the fair grounds are full of them foxes raccoons skunks lemurs thin stray cats dogs wolves nuzzling the boys rubbing

against them and climbing onto their shoulders . . .
a boy shivers and kicks his asshole vibrating as a tail
sprouts out his spine . . .

Trucks pull up and the cops of the world charge out

Billy turns bright red he is fucking teeth bare bleeding this smell billow out his asshole

The cops stop coughing spitting blood from ruptured
lungs

Now the hair is sprouting on him as other boys
stroke his back and pull a tail out his spine bleeding
choking coming gasping into sand foxes in a starlit
desert soft blue electric sky streaked with shooting
stars ejaculating pearls of sperm they show their sharp
little teeth and skitter away

A Lesbian Legion the Fanatical 80 led by Colonel
Wang and the Green Nun vows to destroy the filthy
little beasts before they destroy everything that we
hold dear and sacred . . . And a goodly crowd is there
. . . Mrs Murphy . . . Hamburger Mary . . . Ma-
dame New . . . It's desert county all around the barking of dogs. They are in a steep ravine when suddenly
the barking stops and silence falls like a thunderclap
. . . Robin falls in a fit her tits pop out and she flops
around pissing herself as the girls gather round to
hear her prophetic mutterings . . . "THE DOGS . . .
THE DOGS . . . THE DOGS . . ." She screams out
. . . Now a wall of silent dogs pour down the sides of
the ravine. The girls open up with machine guns and
the dogs keep coming leaping over their fallen com-
rades thousands of silent dogs wave after wave eyes
blazing teeth bare the girls go down screaming ham-
strung torn to pieces as they fall . . . When all the

bitches are dead the dogs roll around on them and lick the blood off each other and fuck and curl up with contented whines and belches and go to sleep.

Audrey opens his eyes in the morning sun. A whine and a scratch at the door. He gets out of bed naked with a hard-on and opens the door. Jerry the red wolf leaps into his arms whimpering nuzzling his teeth against Billy's mouth pumping his sharp red wolf prick against Audrey's stomach as Billy caresses his face and neck nitrous fumes burn out from under his hands the face is half human as he runs his hands down the sides and back and chest fur burns away under his hands the flesh steaming red underneath Billy touches a spot in Jerry's spine and the spine stretches pulling the tail in hands on the buttocks molding them turns his finger in making a human ass hands stroke the animal skin from his penis and balls burning red neon ejaculating youth teeth outlines against the sun. Sharp little teeth say good bye you ladies. Empty house.

Opium Jones there with his glad tidings for Control.

THE "PRIEST" THEY CALLED HIM

"Fight tuberculosis, folks." Christmas Eve an old junkie selling Christmas seals on North Clark Street, the "Priest" they called him. "Fight tuberculosis, folks."

People hurried by grey shadows on a distant wall it was getting late and no money to score he turned into a side street and the lake wind hit him like a knife. Cab stopped just under a street light boy got out with a suitcase thin kid in prep school clothes familiar face the Priest told himself watching from the doorway reminds me of something a long time ago the boy there with his overcoat unbuttoned reaching into his pants pocket for the cab fare. The cab drove way and turned the corner. The boy went inside a building hummm yes maybe; the suitcase was there in the doorway the boy nowhere in sight gone to get the keys most likely have to move fast. He picked up the suitcase and started for the corner made it glanced down at the case didn't look like the case the boy had or any boy would have the Priest couldn't put his finger on what was so *old* about the case, old and dirty poor quality leather and heavy better see what's inside he turned into Lincoln Park found an empty place and opened the case. Two severed human legs had belonged to a young man with dark skin shiny black leg hairs glittered in the dim street light. The legs had been forced into the case and he had to use his knee on the back of the case to shove them out.

"Legs yet" he said and walked quickly away with the case might bring a few dollars to score.

The buyer sniffed suspiciously. "Kinda funny smell about it . . . is this Mexican leather?"

The Priest shrugged.

"Well, some joker didn't cure it." The buyer looked at the case with cold disfavor. "Not even right sure he killed it whatever it is three is the best I can do and it hurts but since this is *Christmas* and you're the *Priest*." $ $ $ He slipped three notes under the table into the Priest's dirty hand.

The Priest faded into the street shadows seedy and furtive three cents didn't buy a bag nothing less than a nickel say remember that old auntie croaker told me not to come back unless I paid him the three cents I owe isn't that a fruit for you blow his stack about three lousy cents.

The doctor was not pleased to see him. "Now what do you *want?* I told you . . ." The Priest laid three bills on the table. The doctor put the money in his pocket and started to scream. "I've had *trouble!* The *people* have been around! I may lose my *license!*"

The Priest just sat there eyes old and heavy with years of junk on the doctor's face.

"I can't write you a prescription!" The doctor jerked open a drawer and slid an ampoule across the table. "That's all I have in the *office!*" The doctor stood up. "Take it and *get out!*" he screamed, hysterical. The Priest's expression did not change and the doctor added in quieter tones: "After all I'm a professional man and I shouldn't be bothered by people like you."

"Is this all you have for me? One lousy quarter g? Couldn't you lend me a nickle?"

"Get out! Get out! I'll call the police I tell you!"

"All right doctor. I'm going now."

Christ it was cold and far to walk rooming house a shabby street room on the top floor these stairs/ cough/the Priest there pulling himself up along the banister he went into the bathroom yellow wood panels toilet dripping and got his works from under the washbasin wrapped in brown paper back to his room get every drop in the dropper he rolled up his sleeve. Then he heard a groan from next door room 18 a Mexican kid lived there the Priest had passed him on the stairs and saw the kid was hooked but he never spoke because he didn't want any juvenile connections bad news in any language and the Priest had had enough bad news in his life heard the groan again a groan he could *feel* no mistaking *that* groan and what it meant maybe had an accident or something any case I can't enjoy my priestly medications with that sound coming through the wall thin walls you understand the Priest put down his dropper cold hall and knocked on the door of room 18.

"*Quién es?*"

"It's the Priest, kid. I live next door."

He could hear someone hobbling across the floor a

bolt slide the boy stood there in his underwear shorts eyes black with pain. He started to fall. The Priest helped him over to the bed.

"What's wrong son?"

"It's my legs *señor* . . . cramps . . . and now I am without medicine."

The Priest could see the cramps like knots of wood there in the young lean legs dark shiny black leg hairs.

"Three years ago I have damaged myself in a bicycle race it is then that the cramps start and . . ."

And he has the leg cramps back with compound junk interest. The old Priest stood there *feeling* the boy groan. He inclined his head as if in prayer went back and got his dropper.

"It's just a quarter g kid."

"I do not require much *señor.*"

The boy was sleeping when the Priest left room 18. He went back to his room and sat down on the bed. Then it hit him like heavy silent snow, all the grey junk yesterdays. He sat there and received the *immaculate fix* and since he was himself a priest there was no need to call one.

"MY LEGS *SEÑOR.*"

attic room and window my ice skates on the wall
the Priest could see the bathroom pale yellow wood
    panels
toilet young legs shiny black leg hairs
"It is my legs *señor.*"
luster of stumps rinses his lavender horizon
feeling the boy groan and what it meant
face of a lousy kid on the doctor's table
I was the shadow of the waxing evenings and strange
    windowpanes.
I was the smudge and whine of missed times in the
    reflected sky
points of polluted water under his lavender horizon
    windowpane
smudge scrawled by some boy cold lost marbles in the
    room
the doctor's shabby table . . . his face . . .
boy skin spreads to something else.
"CHRIST WHAT'S INSIDE?" he screams.
flesh and bones rose tornado
"THAT HURTS."

I was the smudge and whine of missed legs shiny black
    leg hairs
silver paper in the wind frayed sounds of a distant
    city.

THE END

You couldn't say exactly when it hit familiar and
dreary as a cigarette butt ground out in cold scrambled eggs the tooth paste smears on a washstand glass
why you were on the cops day like another just feeling
a little worse than usual which is not unusual at all
well an ugly thing broke out that day in the precinct
this rookie cop had worked a drunk over and the
young cop had a mad look in his eyes and he kept
screaming

"Let me finish the bastard off! He's passed out on
some kinda dope I tell you!"

I've seen that look before and I know what it means:
"cop crazy." When it hits they'll rush out search,
sap, arrest, anyone in sight. We try to cover for them.
"Son, if the cop madness come on you find an old
drunken bum just as quick as you can and let yourself
go."

Well it turned out the rookie has picked the wrong
drunk he was a big ad exec on a spree such a stink
goes up we toss the crazy kid to the wolves and he
draws a stretch and some con beats his brains out in
stir. We can cover for individual cases or write them

off but next day is worse the madness would seize whole precincts for a few minutes during which any one in the tank is beaten to a bloody pulp then the madness drains out and their strength goes with it

"Double whiskey Martin."

"You're a cop kinda early aren't you Clancy?"

Now that Clancy gulped his whiskey and wiped his mouth with a shaky hand.

"I don't know Martin something is happening to me maybe I'm going nuts just to do *anything* Martin, like get up shave and dress well it *hurts* see? I tell myself Clancy anymore from your sap what's all the fuss everyone does these things every day been doing it for years so who am I to start complaining but strength sags from the work I'm doing no blood left in me to sap a sick junkie takes everything I've got to make it to the bus stop and one thought in my mind please God let there be a seat a warm leather seat by the window and when I get to the corner by the precinct and have to lug myself out of the bus?"

"Covered you like the white stuff Clancy?"

"Eh what's that? Give me another Martin."

Martin fills the cop's glass. He leans his grey junkie forearms on the bar. He doesn't care if Clancy sees the needle marks. He doesn't mind shaving and dressing. He speaks calmly.

"Yes it's hitting all of you can't find a taxi in the street or so many they chase a fare up the sidewalk and jerk him in that's another way it hits people go crazy to do something can't just sit here moping gotta DO SOMETHING. I can see it's coming on now Clancy. Yeah you're a cop and you gotta DO SOME-

THING. No that gun won't do you a bit of good. Better put it away. You don't believe in that gun any more Clancy . . . You don't believe in that badge neither nor the work you're doing. What kept you doing it Clancy? It was the feeling you were *on set* knowing you had a part in *the film* and the film covered you just like the white stuff covers a junkie he don't mind shaving and dressing. And you didn't mind doing these things so long as the film covered you why you were on the cops. Well the film isn't there any more Clancy the spring is gone from your sap strength sags from your good right arm cold and wooden your fingers. And what has happened to your pigeons Clancy? You used to be quite a pigeon fancier remember the feeling you got sucking arrests from your pigeons soft and evil like the face of your whiskey priest brother? Where are your pigeons gone to Clancy? Where are their junk rotten souls? rags and tatters of old film . . . Sure Clancy we remember the men you sent up came around later to thank you and the watch the chief gave you when you cracked the Norton case. Time to turn in your cop suit to the little Jew who will check it off in his books . . .

"'Won't be needing you after Friday. Pick up your check at the gate.'

"It was the film held you together, Clancy you *were* the film all the old cop films eating his apple twirling his club . . . The sky goes out against his back."

Unpaid bills unanswered letters each simple task an agony to perform every day a little worse and the worse it got the less was happening as the structure quietly foundered whole apartment blocks phone in to say they won't be coming to the office that day and nobody is there to take the calls. The writer flinches from his typewriter the cop turns sick with the sight of his badge. Tools fall from slack hands plows gather dust in ruined barns. Fanatical sects spring up wrecking whole districts in whirlwind riots. A few minutes later the rioters sit in the wreckage stirring blood with a stick staring into space with dead hopeless eyes. Last twitches of the dying west.

A little fat man was standing by my desk. "I know you. You're the little fat man who gives the explanations in science-fiction stories."

"Yes that's me Bill. Guess you could write my lines for me most of them. You want out of present time do you? Well that's tougher than you thought a whole lot tougher. Time hits the hardest blows. Well I can give you a few hints no more than that mind you and that's against the rule oh yes we have rules. As soon as you work for any organization you have rules and it's a rule that anyone working for any organization cannot be allowed to know the reason for the rules not the real reason . . . present time . . . right now . . . agony to be just here isn't it? Well to begin with let's take a look at people who don't mind being in present time . . . Indians in South America setting fish traps . . . hunting . . . cooking . . . making canoes . . . Well I could go on but you get the picture . . . every object has its place not many objects you see these so-called backward people are *on set*. Present time is a film and if you are *on set* in present time you don't feel present time because you

are *in it*. Well no use trying to duplicate a set like that
in a city of course you can approximate it in your
apartment weed out all the objects not on set but even
if you get your apartment on set where no object jumps
out and kicks you in the stomach sooner or later the
objects move back into random positions and there is
still all outdoors to contend with you trail it back in
with you all those words and sounds and images that
have nothing to do with you . . . All right let's look
at someone else who can make out in present time . . .
A man having breakfast in bed reading letters . . .
He dictates into a dictaphone . . . See what I mean?
He is *rich?* He can buy padding. Someone else will
type the letters he is dictating and pay the bills
and see that the heating works. He can buy exemption
from present time or at least he could until the film
jammed. Now here is someone else doesn't mind being
where he is . . . Martin there cooking up the white
stuff grey shadows on a distant wall . . . So what is
the film made of? JUNK. The more you use the more
you need. And where does that end? Where would it
have ended if we hadn't decided to end it right here
in these United States of America?" He gets up and
paces the room. "What after all is your God? Seen
from a galactic standpoint a little tribal chieftain weak
corrupt a drug addict. Sold out his people justlikethat."
He snaps his fingers. "Yes there is some ground for
the provincial egotism of earth peoples. The planet is
remarkable in many ways . . . the more or less equit-
able temperatures, vegetation, *water* this can be very
important to planets where there is not water like
Mars for instance . . . minerals, oxygen, animal food.

To put it country simple earth has a lot of things other folks might want like the whole planet and maybe these folks would like a few changes made like more carbon dioxide in the atmosphere and room for their way of life. We've seen this happen before right in these United States. Your way of life destroyed the Indians' way of life. Gave them reservations didn't you? Now my own position is ticklish. I'm with the invaders no use trying to hide that and at the same time I disagree with some of the things some of them are doing oh we're not united any more than you are the conservative faction is set on nuclear war as a solution to the personnel problem. Others disagree. Now I don't claim that my motives are one hundred percent humane but I do say if we can't think up anything quieter and tidier than that we aren't all that much better than you earth apes. How many of you people can live without film coverage? How many of you can forget you were ever a cop a priest a writer leave everything you ever thought and did and said behind and walk right out of the film? There is no place else to go. The theater is closed.''

COLD LOST MARBLES

my ice skates on a wall
luster of stumps washes his lavender horizon
he's got a handsome face of a lousy kid
rooming houses dirty fingers
whistled in the shadow
"Wait for me at the detour."
river . . . snow . . . someone vague faded in a mirror
filigree of trade winds
cold white as lace circling the pepper trees
the film is finished
memory died when their photos weather worn points of
polluted water under the trees in the mist shadow of
boys by the daybreak in the peony fields cold lost
marbles in the room carnations three ampoules of
morphine little blue-eyed twilight grins between his
legs yellow fingers blue stars erect boys of sleep
have frozen dreams for I am a teenager pass it on
flesh and bones withheld too long yes sir *oui oui*
craps last map . . . lake . . . a canoe . . . rose tor-
    nado in
the harvest brass echo tropical jeers from Panama
City night fences dead fingers you in your own body
around and maybe a boy skin spreads to something
else on Long Island the dogs are quiet.